This is a work
events are ent

BEYOND T

**First edition. February 7, 2016.**

Copyright © 2016 P.I.Kapllani.

ISBN: 979-8227563897

Written by P.I.Kapllani.

# P.I.Kapllani

# Beyond the Edge

# Beyond the Edge

By

P.I.Kapllani

Published by: \ 0 \N \

2010

Beyond the Edge By Perparim Kapllani
Published by: In Our Words, Inc.
inourwords.ca
Author picture: Abhinav Misra
Cover image: iStockphoto
Editor: Cheryl Antao-Xavier
Library and Archives Canada Cataloguing in Publication
Kapllani, Perparim, 1966-
Beyond the edge : stories / Perparim Kapllani.
ISBN 978-1-926926-04-9
I. Title.
PS8621.A62B49 2010 C813'.6 C2010-907966-3

PRINTED IN CANADA

# Table Of Content

# Dedication

For my mother Shqiponja
    thank you for all you did for me
    and continue to do for me in spite of the distance

# Acknowledgements

When a Russian friend told me that he brought his father's ashes to Canada, I was intrigued by his story and inspired to write "Ashes to Ashes." It is contrary to Albanian tradition to cremate bodies and the thought of this man, an immigrant, bringing the ashes of a loved one to his new country made me think that we all have unusual stories in our lives, some which we bring from a previous life.

All we as writers need to do is observe, listen to the stories of those around us and sit at a computer and imagine our own unique, fascinating storyline.

I once worked in a restaurant where I met a customer, an elderly man in his sixties, who described to me how he witnessed his mother being raped by their Serbian neighbors. He was a nine-year-old boy at the time, but he never forgot that horrific tragedy, which became a daily nightmare for the rest of his life. This was the basis for my story "The Bridge on Bloor." This story was selected for the anthology Canadian Voices Volume I, published by Bookland Press, Toronto.

Years ago I bought a triplex building, where a couple of tenants used to live. One of them died three years ago. He used to live alone, abandoned by his family and he left behind just one living thing, his cat. His death inspired the stories "The Chaser" and "The Talking Clocks."

I remember, when as a kid, I used to live next door to a Cham family, who were expelled from their home in Northern Greece. Their tragic story is the basis for "The Fistful of Dirt." The story is about the Albanian minority in Chameria in

Northern Greece, who even today are not allowed to return to their homes. Over 7000 Albanian Chams were killed by the Greek military led by Zervas, while thousands were expelled from their homes.

"My Sister Hanna' is a dramatic story about a young woman who committed suicide in Albania. Her home was located behind the building of the newspaper where I used to work. It happened that her husband was one of my former high school friends. He told me his story, how he taught his wife to use a gun, the same gun she used to kill herself. I was so deeply affected by that tragedy and my writer's mind worked on the story for years until I came up with "My Sister Hanna," the story of a brother who wants to avenge the death of his sister by killing his brother-in-law whom he blames for the tragedy.

The story "One Dollar" was previously published in a collection of short stories written in the Albanian language Monedha e tmerrshme. This story is not based on actual events, but rather on a folk legend that a wife must be punished if she betrays her husband. In this story, the husband tries to drive his wife out of her mind using a psychological weapon of continually flipping a coin—a coin he took from his wife's lover.

In talking to a Vietnamese friend about gambling, he told me that he lost more than 300 grand at the casino. His wife had divorced him. She took their son with her and now lives with another man. His life was destroyed through gambling, he said, angry and frustrated. I got the story idea for "The Sniper" from him.

These stories are therefore fiction—sadly, sometimes based on actual facts.

I want to thank all these people whose stories inspired me, however unintentionally, to write my stories and go forward with my dream of publishing my second book in English.

Special thanks to Archie D'Cruz, for publishing some of the stories at Chapter & Verse, an online Canadian literary website: chapterandverse.ca. Thanks to Jasmine D'Costa for including "The Bridge on Bloor" in Canadian Voices.

Thank you very much to Cheryl Antao-Xavier, the publisher of In Our Words Inc., who pushed me to go ahead with this collection of short stories.

Perparim Kapllani

Toronto—December 2010

# The Gypsy King

As I walk into the market square framed by many of the same old brick houses I remember from my childhood, the memories flood back so violently I feel weak and almost sink to the flagstoned ground. I have not come home to Elbasan city, to this market square, in seventeen years.

The neighbors will not recognize my face. I hope they don't. I hope they have forgotten the young boy who left the town with a heavy heart, burdened by a terrible guilt. But there will be some who will remember. The Gypsy King will never forget me. How can he when he lives with a daily reminder of me?

It all seems the same. Even the changes are familiar. Each alteration in the neighborhood scenery, in the people who lived there was told to me in detail in Mama's letters. Yes, in the ways that matter nothing has changed. As I walk slowly onwards even the flagstones of the square where I had played so often as a child have a reality steeped in poignant memories. I had walked along this pathway through the square so many times in my mind all these years.

I smell the heavenly aroma of baking even before I see the bakery, the only one we ever went to, that once made my favorite dessert ballakume, a concoction of corn flour, sugar, eggs and butter that is only made here in this city. I have never been able to find it anywhere else in the hundreds of other bakeries I sought out in the many places I visited.

As I walk past the low brick houses, I smell the flowers. I had forgotten this scent of the widow iris flowers, which grew wild in the surrounding hills in my day. Now they seem to blossom everywhere in wild abandon and the air is filled with their scent. This too, though I never looked for it, I have neither seen nor smelled elsewhere.

I catch a glimpse of the Shkumbin River through a break in the trees. Haven't swam there in years. Not since the incident with the Gypsy King. Since that day when our lives changed forever.

I come to a stop before the house where Alma lived. Beautiful Alma, the girl with long black hair had lived here and studied with me at the Thoma Kalefi Elementary School. Mama wrote to tell me when she married two years ago and went to live in Italy with her new family. I had followed Alma's journey to womanhood and out of my life forever—in my mind's eye. Mama's commentary provided the basic details and my own imagination had filled in the story as I wished it had played out. Yes, in my head it had been me who had taken her to Italy and taught her all that I had promised to teach her.

Alma's beautiful eyes aren't peeking out from behind the curtained windows where she would wait for a sight of me. I walk on, having no interest to go there to visit her parents and younger siblings who Mama said still lived there. Her brother Artur is a doctor now and found a job in the capital, Tirana. He won't need my help to learn French ever again. I always wondered if he remembered me. The boy whom he had once worshipped and followed and imitated in every detail must have now faded from his memory. He, a doctor in Tirana, had long since become the envy of his former mentor. What would he say if he knew how many, many times I had walked in his shoes, prayed that I could have had his ambition, his success in life, and especially his "normal" life.

I walk on. Two houses down, the faded blue painted house with its shutters drawn down looks even more forlorn than I remember. Mama wrote that Buba has three kids and doesn't leave home very often. In our childhood games, she used to play the famous pirate queen Teuta, and I would play her husband, King Agron, and we would enact the historical Illyrian Wars all around the market square. I remember how we hid in the bushes, and I had kissed her—twice. She would stand by my side as I fought the Gypsy King.

Always my thoughts came back to the Gypsy King. The garden patch to the side of Buba's house is gone, replaced by a rickety swing set. I walk on.

Marsela, who lived next door, moved with her mother to Vlora city. She was the first girl I had ever kissed. I looked across at the house next to that, where Baci lived. I used to go to his house all the time. Mama wrote that he now works in Greece and never comes back even to visit. When we were kids, his older brother had come back from China filling their home with so many toys and games that every kid in the neighborhood wanted to be invited to play.

Elbasan looks different without the familiar faces of my childhood friends. It looks like a desert, empty and beaten by the cold wind which swoops down off the Krasta hillside. And yet life goes on. It went on even after it ended for me. I cannot seem to focus on the strange faces filling the market square. I look for the familiar faces and don't see even one. The place is like I remember and yet not so in the ways I crave to remember it.

The villagers fill the square selling their wares right in the middle at Bezistan Tree, blocking the local pedestrian traffic with stalls of olive oil, cabbages, beans, fresh garlic and other vegetables laid on the sidewalk with live chickens pecking around.

I walk towards the river, searching faces now, anxious to spot a familiar one. It feels like my friends don't exist except in my memory.

Then I see him.

He is standing outside a spruced up Dea's coffee shop at the corner of the main road leading down to the river. I know him instantly. Even though he, like I, has grown to adulthood. I feel heartsick. My old friend Genti. What will he do? What will he say, how will he react when he sees me?

My heart races as I look across the street at Genti. So real like he is in my dreams, in my nightmares. I could not imagine with accuracy the man grown up from the youth I knew. But even in my dreams he looked big and burly like I see him now. Will he enact the role he does in my dreams, I can hardly think as the mounting dread fills my head. Will he give me a hug and put his arm on my shoulder and invite me to have a coffee at Dea's? Or will he seek revenge for what happened all those years ago.

Seventeen years and I know him still. I don't have to glance at his hand to know it is him. It is Genti, the Gypsy King.

We, the white kids, used to call him "The Gypsy King" and the dark Albanians used to call me "Agron" after the Illyrian king of ancient times. In our war games we would "fight to the death" against each other. How I have relived each of those childhood games millions of times till they are now seared into memory.

My play "castle" was the doors of the archway into Namazgja Center, behind the market square. This building was called the Meat and Fish Shop because it had a popular butchery on the ground floor. The enormous gates made of wood and iron were ideal for our play "castle. " I, as Agron, king of the Illyrians, would hold court inside the gateway and the other white kids, my soldiers, would stand guard behind the doors on the inside. Genti's army made up of ten dark-skinned kids were the "gypsies" who would attack the building's defenses from outside. He, Genti, was called the "Gypsy King."

"Remember when we used to break our makeshift swords all the time?" I said to Genti thousands of times in my imaginary conversations with him in the years since I left. We both would laugh and lean back against the "castle" archway and watch the pretty girls go by on the sidewalk. The same pretty girls who we knew as kids, giggling and glancing coyly at us as they would do when Genti and I in our makeshift armor strutted around our "battlefield." So many times had I dreamt different scenes playing out on that "battleground." Sometimes in those dreams Genti and I would be kids, sometimes we would be grown men. But always, we stood side by side as friends, not foes. But always I awoke to a reality far away from this place.

My hometown memories are sweet and light and bring the only smiles to my face when I dream of the innocent times, mostly with Genti beside me. Genti's people were the swarthy-complexioned Albanians who lived in our city. Many gypsies used to live in our neighborhood in those days and though the adults rarely mixed, the kids would play together. The war game was just one of the many games we would play together. I remember in clear detail how we used to make up our costumes, nailing our wooden swords together from cast off planks and building our armor from the stolen lids of garbage bins. The girls used to wear crowns made of flowers on their heads, pretending to be the Illyrian damsels or princesses who walked this land more than 2000 years ago.

Suddenly I realize Genti has seen me. He is standing stock-still trying to believe his eyes as recognition vies with disbelief. My heart stops beating, my throat constricts and I begin to feel lightheaded from lack of oxygen. In the terrible few seconds that pass when I agonize over his possible reactions to seeing me, I fight to stay put and not run. Run back to my self-imposed exile.

But no. I will not do that. I will stand and see this through if only to bring about an end to my own mental torture.

Slowly, as in slow motion, I raise my hand in a mock military salute. How often as a kid he had taunted me for that modern-day salute I would give him in our battle scenes, which he argued no soldier of the Middle Ages would even know about. As our play swords were usually broken into pieces by the end of battle scenes, the hand salute was all we could give one another at the conclusion of our games, so I would insist stubbornly on compliance with that protocol. Good-natured as he always was, Genti would laughingly return the salute with a mock flourish.

As my trembling hand touches my forehead, the recognition hits home instantly. Genti gave a huge bellow—deeper and gruffer and louder than the one I remember but with the same heartiness of old. He had always been strong and well-built as a child, now I see he has packed on pounds over the muscle to have considerable girth especially around his waist. But his bulk does not seem to stop him as he launches himself across the street, the biggest, hugest grin on his face.

"Damnation, look who has shown up," he bellows, causing quite a stir in the street. "Damned devil Agron, you bastard, is it really you? Where the hell have you been? Get over here and explain yourself, you King of Idiots. I'll be damned if it isn't you."

I don't think he even remembers my real name. He had always called me "Agron" or its short form "Goni" after the character I played in our childhood games.

Everything happens so fast. In my dreams and nightmares his reactions to the sight of me had always been enacted in slow motion. Now it seems hardly half a second since I stand with my arm still raised, my hand still to my forehead, trembling so violently that had he not reached me so quickly and grabbed hold of me, enveloping me in a bear hug and lifting me off my feet, though I stood at least six inches taller than him, I know for sure I would have collapsed to the ground.

My head buzzed agonizingly. I want to hear each word he utters, but I can just see his lips moving, his grin wide, open-mouthed, baring his huge, yellowing teeth, his unruly moustache sprouting wildly on either side of his mouth. The noise in my head from the blood rushing to my brain is too loud for me to hear anything outside my head. I cannot hear him. I cannot speak. I know not how long we hold this position, me suspended off the ground looking down at his face, ugly, red-blotched, but so, so dearly loved and dearly missed.

Finally, he sets me down with a thud and his hands move to my shoulder. I dare not look at that left hand. I dare not. But my eyes are drawn to it, as it lies on my right shoulder. He sees my glance and his face softens.

"That is why you went away, isn't it," he says gruffly. "You confounded fool, King of Fools, I knew that was why you went away. Tell me I'm right. Tell me, Agron, King of Nincompoops, did you run away like a yellow-bellied missish girl because of this?"

With that he holds up his mangled left hand in my face. My eyes fixed on his hand and saw clearly what I had imagined so many times in my mind, the strong hand, with the two fingers, the ring finger and the middle finger missing, the flesh mottled and badly set over the gap.

I cannot speak. I did not have to. He saw the pain, the torture, the living dread in my eyes that I did not bother to conceal.

He had always been the emotional one, crying when he was hurt and never giving a damn if anyone thought him "soft" because of it. Now I saw his eyes, less than two feet from mine, fill with tears of understanding.

"You stupid fool," he finally says in a voice that shook, "You didn't even give me a chance to tell you it didn't matter. It was an accident. You are like my brother. That's what matters. That's what always mattered. Not this."

With the last two words he presses his left hand into my face. Then that hand and arm went around my neck and I was pulled into another bear hug that again knocks the air out of me. This time, my own arms go around him in a grip of desperation that he cannot help but feel.

"Genti," I can hardly hear myself speak, "how I prayed you would react this way."

"And how the fuck did you think I was going to react anyway?" growls Genti. We are now seated across from each other at a table in Dea's coffee shop.

I can still hardly believe we are actually sitting together. How many times I'd dreamt this. And it was finally happening. My eyes devour him. I want to reach out and touch him, grab his mangled hand and wipe away the scars, pull at the flesh to create new fingers to replace the ones I had lopped off all those years ago. If I could take anything back in life, it would be that stupid, careless, thoughtless moment when wanting to "win" a battle I was "losing" I had lashed out at him with my makeshift sword. Only that time, that god-awful damnable time, the makeshift sword was not made of the usual cardboard or sticks or sawn-off planks. It was a butcher's long knife, rusted and discarded carelessly in the pile of garbage near the gateway. I had found it and gleefully wielded it like a medieval madman. Carelessness on the part of so many that would change forever the lives of the two of us sitting across from one another.

"I didn't know what to think," I hardly recognize my voice. It sounds so different from the youthful, vulnerable voice I have had in my head when I carried out these imaginary conversations with Genti. "All I remember was your father yelling at me at the hospital, my mother yelling at me at home. Everyone yelling at me that I had killed you. Maimed you for life. Ruined your life forever.

"God, Genti, if there was any way I could have taken that moment back," the raw pain rasps at the back of my throat.

"Damn you, Goni," his arm shoots out and playfully cuffs me on the shoulder. "You're freaking me out with this weird talk. You've been moping about that all these years? I cursed you for the first few months as I had to learn how to do things without those blasted fingers, but then life just went on. Why did you have to run away? I missed you more than those damned fingers, you moron." He cuffs me again, this time harder.

Then the dam broke and I cry like I have never allowed myself to cry in all those seventeen years. All those years when I relived that fateful moment in our childhood millions and millions of times. The words spill out, muffled in sobs so that he has to lean forward almost touching my face to hear them. I tell him everything. How his mutilation at my hand has filled my life like a death sentence. How I watched him in my mind's eye, growing up, learning how to do everything with the other hand. When I tell him how I feared as he grew to manhood he would dread the horror women would feel at the sight of his mutilation, he looks astounded and then throws back his head and guffaws so loudly people from outside the coffee shop peer in to see what is going on.

"Now that is a damned fool notion if ever I heard one," he wipes away tears of laughter and a deeper emotion. "Nothing ever stopped the women from making eyes at me. Mutilation, my ass. They love it. Just adds to the macho appeal, my boy." He laughs heartily, but I can see that my obsession with his injury all these years has deeply affected him.

"I tried to get in touch with you," he says, "but your mother kept scuttling off every time I approached her. I think she thought I was going to ask her for compensation or something. Same with those damned white friends of yours. Suddenly no one wanted to play with us. Not that any of us wanted to play with those snotty wimps after you had gone."

He stops talking and looks at me, "You going away changed everything. No one was the same again. Elbasan wasn't the same again. That incident became a huge issue. People talked about revenge attacks. They stayed away from our people. Took a year before I could walk these streets without anyone expecting me to come chasing after them with a pick axe. Ha! Can't say I didn't want to live up to their expectations. Assholes the lot."

"My mother wrote to me," I say. "She told me all about what was happening here. I often felt as though I was still living here."

"She should not have sent you away," he says gruffly. "That was the wrong way to deal with something like that. I can see you're all messed up in your head over this. Wouldn't have happened if you had stuck around. We'd have gotten back together sooner and the whole thing would have been forgotten."

"She did what she thought was right."

"What made you come back? She died a while back. She went somewhere else to die, I remember. I kept an eye on your house now and then just to see if you'd come back."

"She came to live with me when she took ill. When she saw how affected I was by what happened all those years ago, she made me promise I'd come back and lay the ghosts to rest after she died."

"And so have you come to lay the ghost of past deeds to rest?" he is laughing again, but his eyes watch me. "You're not going to finish me off by lopping off my bloody head now, are you? Okay, okay, bad joke I know. But what did you expect would happen?"

"I played out so many scenes of what could possibly happen," I say sheepishly. "In most of them, you lopped off my head."

"I've a good mind to do just that for wasting all these great years of growing up with whining about a childish act that went wrong," he says. "Damn you, Goni, what a bloody waste of our lives. Never had another friend like you. Bunch of bloomin" ninnies in this damned place."

He could not have said anything better to me more guaranteed to bring a smile to my face. I have almost forgotten how to smile. I think he knew, because he rises, gives me a hard whack on the back, his eyes misting over with emotion.

"Now stop this drivel talk and let's get out of this sissy tea shop and go get some real man drinks. They've got this bar down by the far end of the square, opened after you'd left. Good Elbasan brew they have there."

I rise, look him in the eye with great emotion brimming in my own and I see that he understands.

Slowly he raises his hand in salute. I raise mine in a return salute. The seventeen-year standoff—all of it played out in my own head— is over.

King Agron is once again at peace with the Gypsy King.

# One Dollar

The front door of the apartment slammed open and crashed to the floor. Dan Bala was holding a kitchen knife in his hand as he slowly approached his wife Klara.

Albert lay naked on their bed turning as grey as the décor around him. The silence was eerie, like in the cemetery down the road. For awhile none of them moved, Dan's stare now fixated on the naked man lying on his bed, who just stared back at him. Klara's eyes were fixed on Dan.

In his mind Dan began to work out every detail of what would follow. Klara's head would be lopped off. Albert's ribs broken. And for him, it would be on to a cold prison cell where he would spend the rest of his life for their murders. He even felt the relief the revenge would bring as this nightmare of deception ended with the discovery of its reality. In his mind he heard the gossip that would spread like wildfire through the Albanian community in the Marlee area of Toronto, as the news of Klara's betrayal leaked out. It was at that thought that he lowered the knife.

Hate flared in his eyes.

"Take out whatever money you have in your pockets," he ground out, eyes boring into Albert, who was still on the bed.

Albert Vreshta jumped out of the bed and grabbed his pants searching frantically for something in his pockets. Shivering and sweltering, Vreshta found one dollar and gave it to Dan Bala, his ex-boss and close friend for more than five years. Dan took the coin in his hand, his eyes shifting to Klara.

"Now, get the hell out of my house," he spat out with a violent gesture towards the door. He waited till Vreshta grabbed his clothes and ran out of the room, through the living room and out of the apartment.

Bala held up the dollar coin, arm outstretching slowly till it was leveled in the space between him and Klara. Their eyes were drawn to focus on the coin.

"This, woman, is the worth of your betrayal," his voice was quiet, but menacing. "This is what it was all worth. This is what you are worth."

The couple had come to Canada seven years ago. Dan worked hard and when he set up his construction business he spent long hours at work. Klara spent most of her days inside their apartment, watching television.

The loneliness and isolation had taken its toll in her increasingly unkempt appearance. The inner pain clouded her eyes with deep shadows. She had stopped waiting for him to come back from work, for Dan was always late and had no energy for conversation after those long work hours. She was not a real wife to him she knew. She hadn't been for a long, long time.

Now as she looked at the controlled rage in his eyes, blazing at her from behind the dollar coin that he held up, she knew that this showdown had been coming. It was expected, even perhaps anticipated. It got him to notice her at least. Her betrayal was natural, a woman's need to feel wanted. Yet the reasons for her infidelity kept slipping away from her mind even as she frantically tried to hold them up, throw them in his face.

"His neglect of me is to blame for this betrayal," her mind frantically formed reasons for her defense, to counter any accusations he would make. The terror began to slowly consume her.

"Your secret boyfriend had nothing special," finally Dan spoke. "I don't understand. Why did you betray me with him? He is not more handsome than me...Not taller, not a muscle man. He doesn't even know how to speak properly. He is not rich. For gods' sake, he is my fucking worker. What do you see in him? If you betrayed me for him, for nothing, then you have lost everything...for nothing."

Klara could not speak. She wanted to spew out the accusations, but the words would not come. She wanted to explain how things had deteriorated between them, how she was always alone, eyeing their empty bed with sorrow. How many times she prepared dinners for two, but Dan never showed up to eat with her. When he finally came, he wolfed the food down without a word and went straight to bed and was asleep almost immediately. Night after night. She wanted to cry out about the many times she was waiting for him in their bed, surrounded by the four blank walls. She wanted to tell him that he had forgotten her.

The words still would not come. How often she had wanted to ask him if he had another family. She was jealous and angry for all these years, but never said anything, the words hanging in the air around her during those few minutes in the early mornings at breakfast before he left for work.

It was over a year now that she realized she didn't have the willpower to survive this new reality of their failed marriage. That was when Klara had lost hope. The sun in her life had turned black, the hope and memories of their earlier days of marriage began to fade. When she met Albert, Dan's friend, their family friend, their only friend for the longest time, her need for attention made her too vulnerable. Albert was there for her, where Dan was not, had not been for too, too long.

The coin was beginning to blur with the blackness of hell, the black hole of hell where his wife would be damned infinitely. He could see the blurred image of her beyond the coin being sucked into the cold metal to disappear forever. Damned forever for her betrayal. His rage began to subside into cold, dark hatred.

The look in his eyes was one she had never seen. The terror became numbing.

"Put your dress on," he said to her and backed up to a chair, lowering himself into it slowly, menacingly. His head had been buzzing for awhile now and voices began steadily echoing, arguing, dueling inside his brain, pulling and pushing him in and out of reality. He wanted to scream at her again, "why did you do it?"

He began tossing the coin in the air.

From that day onwards, every time he was home, and he was home for lunch every day now, in the mornings, at lunch time and at dinner, he would sit watching her, take out the coin from his pocket and begin tossing it in the air. The coin would dance in the air, fall and spin on the table, the spin crazy at times, then slapped down to quietness with the full weight of his palm or the back of his hand.

The coin formed circles in the air, circles which were like a lasso forming loops that seemed to come closer and closer to her becoming nooses around her throat. She began to feel she was that coin, destined to be captive because of her shame under his vindictive hand.

Dan said not a single word to her in the days that followed. The spinning dollar coin began to consume her and push her beyond reason. His silence and his unsmiling face became even more menacing. The coin became dominating, filling her life, speaking to her. She began to hear its metallic ring sounding out words, condemning her.

"I am shrinking your skin, making it yellow. I am thickening your eyebrows. I am covering your body with wild hair and putting layers of fat around your neck. I am pushing you to lose your identity; pushing you to remember who you are and what you have done. This is your true worth. One dollar."

As time went on, every time Dan tossed the loonie in the air, the effect on Klara was startling. For a while it was as though a pack of wolves began howling in her head the moment he drew the coin out of his pocket. She wondered if Dan was howling or if she was going mad. Her days became grey with the monotony of a life that had become centered on a spinning coin, nothing seemed to matter but that damned spinning coin. It became a permanent refrain to her life. It had become big and constant and consuming. Such a little insignificant thing was now holding her captive in its spell.

Klara Bala was surprised in the beginning, when Dan began tossing that dollar in the air with such regularity. She thought he would eventually give up and stop the mental torture. But as the days went on and the cruel ritual became regular three times a day, she knew it was a constant reminder of that day of unfaithfulness. He was playing a mind game. A cruel and dangerous mind game. Dangerous because she did not know how he meant to end it. Cruel because she knew in spite of her will to ignore it, he had drawn her into its spell tormenting her with the thrice daily reminder of her infidelity.

"Why does he do this? Why doesn't he scream and yell or hit me? That would be better than this. If he wants to take revenge, he could do it in so many different ways, so much quicker and be done with it. Maybe he is playing this cat and mouse game to drive me insane. I wish, I pray to God, this will end and soon. May he forget it and forgive me and stop this craziness, this insanity. I should speak up, throw the blame where it belongs, blame him for what happened. If I did something wrong, it's partly his fault also. Why should the woman be blamed for cheating, when men who cheat say they do it because of their wives' neglect of them. He has neglected me. I want to scream that at him."

Klara looked at herself in the mirror. The two violet circles around her eyes were growing bigger, spreading and darkening. They stood out dark and haunted against her pallor. Her forehead was growing wrinkled and grey appeared in her beautiful dark hair. In a few short months since that day she had aged considerably.

Whenever she tried to approach him the loonie began its tortuous spinning, pushing her to stay back, mesmerizing her. One day she thought to steal it from his pocket, while he was asleep, but she could not find it in his pocket. He had it under his pillow. Sometimes she saw him holding the coin tight in his hand, as he slept. They were not sleeping together anymore. He had not slept in their bed since the day he saw Albert in it. She was scared to sleep with him in the same room.

Five months had passed before her nightmare ended as suddenly as it had started that awful day when Dan had crashed their bedroom door to the ground. She had then taken refuge in her room, in her bed, shutting her mind to the sight of him and that damned coin.

He never forgave her. Every one of the many times he seemed to relent became moments of false hope, when she thought that he had forgiven her, when his eyes lost that hard look. But when the hope rose into her eyes, his would harden with a coldness that would chill her to the bone.

Then one morning he came into the kitchen as she moved about listlessly getting their breakfast, trying to ignore him even as her mind waited intently for the familiar sounds. She waited to hear it begin, the scraping of a hand into a pocket. The click of a nail against a coin. Then the staccato sounds of clicking, slapping, clicking as the coin was tossed, caught, tossed, again and again and again.

She strained for the sounds and the silence becoming its own torture. In her mind she knew: he wants me to turn around and look at him. Then he will start tossing it again. I know he will. But in spite of herself, in spite of the many times he had waited silent like this, she still turned and looked at him.

Dan was looking at her. The hard look was not there. At least not yet. He had the coin in his hand. Keeping his eyes on her, he raised his hand, but instead of tossing the coin upwards into the air as he had done so many thousands of times in the last five months, he flicked it sideways and out through the open window.

In the quiet of the early morning, they heard the sharp clinks as the coin hit and bounced off a pile of tin cans stored beneath the window. The dogs snoozing outside the back door were startled, yelped and scuttled away.

Dan turned and walked out.

# The Bridge on Bloor

The silhouette of a man appears against the night sky on the Bloor bridge, where it spans the Humber River, a short distance from the heart of Toronto.

The ghostly figure lifts his arms up toward the sky and an eerie wail soars through the air, echoing off the banks of the Humber below. The wails turn to screams and rants in a language strange to the few who hear it.

Another ghost-like figure of a man approaches rapidly to the left of the silhouette, his eyes gleaming in the dark, fixated on the wailing creature. The silhouette continues to scream, pausing only to listen to the echo of his cry bouncing back from the night shadows.

The man is short and bespectacled. He appears to be cringing at the horrible sound, yet reluctantly drawn towards the phantom figure. The man feels his body shaking and he is not sure whether it is from fear or the intense cold.

From a distance the figure of the man is seen stopping before the silhouette.

"Hey! Who are you? Why are you crying? Can I help you?"

The silhouette is seen turning towards the man, whose small figure seems to shrink even further, as though he has been caught witnessing a private moment of unguarded pain.

"Why did you scream, sir?" asks the man. "Who are you? Why do you come here to scream into the night?"

The words seem to resound in the silence, the echo seeming to mock the man. The phantom puts his finger to his lips and indicates silently that the man should listen to the echo of his words, off the bridge and through the night.

"Do you hear the echo?" he asks. Without waiting for an answer he continues, "Echolocation is a method of sense perception through which some animals self-orientate, find obstacles, communicate with other animals and find food. I use the echolocation method to orientate myself in the dark of night. That's why I scream, with all my strength."

As he says that he lets out a wrenching scream, terrible in the intensity of pain it communicates. He waits for the echo to die down then continues to speak as if there had been no pause.

"My name is Desmodus Ruphus and I am like a bat in the night. I am lost, without a soul. I come here to orientate myself. For months now I have come and stood in the middle of this big bridge of Toronto, on Bloor Street and cry aloud into the night air. I seek answers, resolution to pain."

"Where have you come from?" the man asks.

"Bania Luka in Bosnia."

The silhouette pauses then begins to tell the man his story. The words fall from his mouth like a release of pent-up emotion.

"I left my homeland when I was 12 years old travelling on a freight train straight to Croatia. This was after a group of Serbians attacked our home and killed my father, my grandmother, my grandfather, two aunts and my uncle. They burned down my house and stole our cow."

He pauses and looks over the parapet of the bridge down into the dark waters far below, seeming to relive those painful events.

"I left Croatia when I was 21 years old. I stayed awhile in Italy and after seven months left for Canada.

"I have never been back since. I don't want to go back there.

"I could not sleep last night. I see my mother in my dreams. She is crying. I see the same horrible nightmare several times a month, the same dream for years. I relive that time, when my Serbian neighbors came into my house. I cannot forget after all these years the wild man who tore off my mother's clothes with such force. I was shocked and totally paralyzed with fear. He raped my mother in front of my eyes. I felt shame, shaking and shivering with terror and anger. I don't remember how long I stayed bewildered and helpless, watching my mother moaning and groaning under that man. Those minutes seemed like hours.

"I ran out of the house and went into the backyard and pulled a stick off a fence and went back into the house. I attacked that man with the stick and only then did he stop raping my mother. He boxed her ears so violently then, that she was deaf for the rest of her life. She died two years later.

"That terrible incident changed me forever as a human being. I have kept my head down all my life. It has consumed me. When I cannot bear the thoughts anymore, I come here and start screaming, trying to release the pain and terror of that night. I feel some release then. The ball of emotions that rises to stick in my throat only goes away then."

The phantom turns and looks at the man. "Now you know why I come here and stand screaming into the darkness on the Bloor bridge," he says.

The man listens silently, wiping his tears with the back of his left hand.

"Are you ever going to go back to Bania Luka?" he asks the phantom. "To lay the demons in your head to rest?"

"I can't go back. I am scared of myself. I might start killing everybody, whoever comes in front of me, or I might get killed myself. My Serbian neighbors are still there. They know what I saw. There is nothing else for me to do. The only relief for me is to come here sometimes and release the pain with this screaming. I scream out loud in order to release my pain."

The man shakes his head and looks helpless as the phantom sobs in misery.

"You must release this pain once and for all," says the man. He waves at the phantom as if to say throw your problems away over the bridge into the waters. "You must move on with your life."

The phantom looks hard at him then asks the man to help him rid himself of his torturous thoughts.

"Help me to get rid of this pain by screaming at the darkness below. I have no other way of releasing this pain. Help me, please."

He puts his hands around his mouth and lets out a series of blood-curdling screams. The man does the same and screams into the night. Their screams are so loud, that the stars in the sky seem to tremble with the impact of the echoes. The phantom screams louder than the man. Then the man screams louder than the phantom. Like wolves, wild and mournful, they pour their hearts out over the earth, releasing pent up frustrations and pain.

Their eyes light up like madmen. The phantom screams on and on, made crazy by the magic of the night. Then he falls back, spent and at peace at last.

The man looks down over the parapet of the bridge, a great distance below into the dark waters of the river. He is silent. His eyes rivet onto a patch of moonlight on the water in the shape of a woman's face, its eyes haunting like that of the phantom's.

The eyes of the woman are smiling up at him, as the image slowly fades into the gentle waves of the Humber River.

# Ashes to Ashes

I dug up my father's grave and removed what was left of him. I then had his remains cremated and put his ashes in a wooden urn shaped like a bottle. I carried the urn under my arm to my home where I then placed it in a suitcase as part of my luggage. I had accomplished my mission and was ready to return home.

My name is Mark Shkoza. I am forty-one years old. Three years ago I left my homeland Albania, a small country located in the Balkan Peninsula. My destination was Canada. I left never to return.

I still don't speak English very well but can communicate enough for my needs. I worked double shifts when I first arrived in Canada. I had nobody—no family, no friends—and it seemed like I was running, trying to lose my mind. That's why I came back to Albania. I got only one week off work and I came on this special mission, a very important mission, to bring my dead father back with me.

I didn't really know why I took this decision, to exhume my father's body and bring his ashes over here, close to where I live. Maybe it was the loneliness or maybe I was afraid that there would be no one to take care of his grave.

I had heard on an Albanian community TV channel in Toronto that vandalism at graveyards "back home' was common. In one case the police had found some grave tiles lying on the floor of the public washroom at the graveyard. When I had heard that news I began to vomit, the anger and pain robbing me of my appetite as well. I imagined those marble tiles, which had covered the grave of my dead father, lying in the washroom under the feet of those peeing monsters who had stolen them. I felt like I was the one lying on the floor under those dirty shoes, consumed by their callousness.

The thought made me sick and I went to the washroom time after time to throw up as I was sticking my fingers into my throat to keep vomiting to rid myself of this strange nausea. But it was in vain. The anger and the nausea would not go.

I became obsessed with the thought of my father's grave, his last resting place, being desecrated by vandals. I had to go bring him back with me.

When I went back to Albania for him, I found his grave covered with grass and wild blueberry shrubs. His picture, set in ceramic tile had been placed at the head of his grave and it was now cracked and I saw that the marble tiles that had lain on top of his gravesite had indeed been taken away like many of the other graves.

When I arrived back in Canada, I made arrangements to inter my father's ashes in the cemetery nearby. As I arrived with the urn containing my father's ashes tucked under my arm, clutching tightly on to it, I felt as though my father was roaring inside the urn. I became scared, helpless. I began to feel strange and hallucinate. It had to be a hallucination, it could not be true! For in front of me, I saw a giant penguin on the ice, playing a drum with his flippers.

"Bum, bum, bum, bum, bum," the drum sounded mournful.

The penguin's eyes were boring into me like a laser beam. I was still holding the urn. My mouth gaped open and my breath almost stopped. I felt the surface of my tongue dry out and my spit stuck like a ball in my throat, choking me. I tried to breathe, but the emptiness of my chest was burning me so bad, like a parched desert. My eyes were fixed on the icy mirage that was beating the drum with a mournful, menacing sound.

Bum bu bu bum, bum bu bu bum, bu bum! The drum sounded then stopped and the penguin spoke.

"I am Angel Israfil. This is the end of the world for you," the penguin said. It was freezing cold but I was suddenly sweating. I wiped at my tired eyes with the sweaty palm of my hand. I thought that I was dreaming. I looked around. I was standing in the Mount Pleasant Cemetery, which was blanketed in snow even though it was March. There were bits of ice, freezing rain, falling on my head and those of the few people in the cemetery. The ice was like needles piercing me like angry pellets.

I had come with the urn that I had brought my father's ashes in to bury in this cemetery. I knew that I would be burying my father in this foreign country, among these people he never knew. But now I would have the chance to visit him at least once a week and I will sleep well without being afraid that vandals would disrespect his grave and steal his marbled tiles.

"You are wrong!" said the angel, as though he could read my thoughts. "Your father will haunt you in your dreams and he will ask you to take him back, where he belongs, close to his own father."

I started to shake. My rough black hair stood up like pricks on my head. This vision of the Angel Israfil was saying something that I had not thought of before. That I had taken my father away from his own father who was left behind, far away, in Albania. My grandfather's grave was located a few feet away from my father's grave. I did not think about that at all in my obsession to take my father away from there.

I thought of my grandfather. I remember him coughing so hard and spitting into a dirty glass. His long stories, those wonderful tales filled with strange characters, such as Nastradin and the Bald Man had captivated me. I felt a momentary stab of pain that he had been left behind without my father, but his grave was less exposed to thieves than my father's grave. My grandfather's grave was much older and not covered with marble. It was sunken in the ground and the wooden nameplate at the head of the gravesite was damaged by the rain and exposed to the sun and the wind. He was forgotten even by the vandals. They couldn't harm his grave any more than the elements had already. They could only step on his grave, over the dried and cracked soil that covered his resting place.

My own father's image on the other hand was forever young because his relatives had put a picture of him on his grave, an old picture of when he was a student in the Soviet Union and had fallen in love with a beautiful Russian girl, called Valentina, in Leningrad.

The penguin beat harder on the drum as if to draw my attention back. No one else seemed to see it. The undertakers took the urn from me carefully and placed it in a vault, alongside other urns. Then they left discreetly to leave me to mourn quietly. As I relinquished it, I had the feeling that it shook as if something was moving inside it.

I turned to the angel Israfil to ask what he was trying to say to me. He was not playing his drum anymore. I stood before my father's vault silently for what seemed like hours. Suddenly the silence was broken and I heard my father's voice for the first time coming from inside the urn.

"Mark. Why did you do this?" he asked.

"Because I missed you," I whispered, confused.

"Death doesn't mean anything," he answered. "I am always with you."

"I felt alone. I had nobody to talk to. I work most of the time and the rest of the day I stay at home. My evenings were becoming a torture. I didn't know what to do."

"It is your life; I can't help you, my son. You must find help from the living."

I was silent. His voice rumbled again from the dust inside the bottle.

"Why don't you marry," he asked.

I was shivering. I could see his ashes rolling in circles inside of the wooden urn, like the sand on the seashore stirred by the wind.

"I don't want to get married for now. I have got to work for some time. You left me nothing. I have to work to earn my living." I pointed my finger accusingly at the urn, "Besides, I want someone familiar here with me. I visited your grave every week in Albania. I miss that."

The ashes in the urn began to stir violently.

"How can you bring me like this to this strange land? A handful of earth from my grave, yes, you had the right to bring that here, at the end of the world. But how dare you disturb my resting place? You burned me? It's not in our tradition to do these things! Where is the Shkumbin River of my hometown? Where is the strong wind that blows down from the Krasta's hill? And the grave which my brother laid for me with tiles. And I'll miss my sisters, who visited my grave."

"There is freedom here. Safety. They will not disturb your grave here," I defended my actions. "Alright, I am not going to place you in this public cemetery. I'll bring you home, into my home."

"No! Take me back, now!" his voice said from inside the urn. "You must live with the living, not focus on the dead."

I thought of him dying as a young man. I was ten years old, when the police came to my elementary school and told me that my father had been killed on the street. I didn't remember many details of that day in February 1977. I just know that I remained close to his memory all this while.

"I cannot rest in peace here on this alien soil. I am forgotten ashes in this urn in a foreign land. You may as well throw my ashes to the wind so I can go back to the earth where I belong to. You hear me?"

"I am an immigrant in this country. Who else do I have to talk to? I need you."

"You have grown to be selfish, son. You are thinking just of yourself. How can you remove my bodily remains, burn them and bring them here. Just so you have company? Live with the living."

"Be quiet!" I yelled. Some people in the cemetery turned around to look at me uneasily.

I was so nervous and angry. I wanted to throw his ashes to the wind like he asked. But I couldn't do that. My father was my father after all and I loved him even after death. Even though I was so young when he died, I had loved him and had always been loyal to his memory.

"Why did you leave me, father?" I heard myself sobbing the words I had never uttered before. "Who killed you? Tell me, who killed you, so I can take revenge for your death. I want to face your killer and tell him what he took away from me."

The words that came from the urn next were the most damning I had ever heard.

"You killed me, son. I knew I couldn't afford to take care of you, so I took my life. You pushed me to kill myself." There was a pause, then, "Now you have brought me here, far away from home so you kill me for the second time."

I felt desperate. This had not worked out the way I had thought it would. My father did not want to be with me. He wanted to be free. Free in his home country. Albania. Not here with me in Canada.

I decided then that I would take his ashes back to Albania and bury him in the spot from where I had taken him. I knew his spirit would rest easy there and I would have someone to come back to visit.

# My Sister Hanna

My sister Hanna committed suicide three days ago. I buried her yesterday. I slowly pull the trigger of the AK47 rifle, pointing it at Roland, her husband. I am convinced that it was he who had pushed my sister over the edge to commit suicide.

"Put your hands against the wall," I cried out at him.

Roland puts his hands on the wall and waits.

"What's your last wish before you go straight to hell?"

"Brother, I am really sorry for what happened."

"I am not your brother. How did she get the gun?"

"I bought it. I bought it for 200 dollars."

"What did you need the gun for?"

"Two trespassers broke into our house. After that Hanna was always scared and I thought it would be better for us to buy a gun to protect ourselves."

"Then what happened?"

"I was coming home late most of the time, so Hanna became suspicious that I was cheating on her. I was running from one job to the other. I had to take care of my business, that's why I was spending more time at the restaurant. Hanna became jealous. When I had finished working for the day, she was waiting for me, no matter how late I was. She was asking me weird questions, driving me crazy."

"Driving you crazy, huh? Now she is dead."

"Yeah, I feel horrible."

"Why was she jealous of you? Were you cheating on her?"

Roland was silent.

"Answer me, were you cheating on her?"

Yes. I was cheating." He almost screamed at me.

"With the same waitress, who works at your restaurant, right?"

"Yes, yes."

"How did my sister find out about your affair?"

"She never found out about it. She kept asking me questions. That's all."

"What kind of questions?"

"Where was I? Why I was coming late? Why didn't I come home early? I was trying not to let it get to me. I kept smiling at her, even though I was pissed most of the time. I was trying to be cool. I never imagined that she was obsessing about it so much. I was trying to forget about all this tension at home by getting busy with my daily work. I didn't even have time to deal with her feelings."

"Did she see you with the other woman?"

"No, but she accused me of having another family. Hanna was becoming more and more upset and angry when I came home late. She felt unsafe here alone. That's why I made my house safe with this weapon."

"Yeah, your house became a safe haven," I ground out sarcastically. "Do you really think you made it safe? Leaving that gun with her in that condition?"

"Thieves came into our house and tried to steal as much as they could, but I was there at that time, so they escaped without getting anything. I built a very high fence after that and I put barbed wire rolled over it and I cemented small pieces of glass on top of the wall. You know, life is different around here. All our neighbors came from far away, from the rural areas. Huh. It is no longer safe."

"You decided to buy the gun, since those thieves came into your house, right?"

"I didn't realize that the gun would change our lives forever."

"What kind of gun did you buy?"

"Automatic gun, an AK47."

"The one I am pointing at you right now?"

"Yes!"

"How did she learn how to use the gun?"

"I taught her how to use it. I never realized that she would kill herself with the same gun one day."

"Where did you train her?"

"I trained her in our backyard."

"What did you teach her exactly?"

"Aiming the AK47, trigger squeeze, breath control and follow through."

"When did the lesson start?"

"Six months ago. But she was having nightmares before I bought the gun. Why are you asking me all these questions?"

"Because I want to know everything. How you planned to kill her. How you executed it.

You were training your own wife how to shoot even when you knew she was suffering from mental stress and had recurring nightmares? How many bullets did you buy?"

"I bought three cartridges with ten bullets each, just in case, if she ever wanted to use them, in order to protect our house from burglars."

"What is the caliber in millimeter for this rifle?"

"The caliber is 7.62 mm."

"That is going to be the size of the hole that I'm going to make in your head. What is the muzzle's velocity?

"830 meter per second."

"That's the speed of the bullet that will go through your fucking brain. Now tell me, what is the magazine's capacity, how many rounds can you fit in one cartridge?"

"You can fit ten bullets, sir."

"Don't sir me!" I yelled at him. "There are nine bullets, actually, because one was used by Hanna. Nine bullets will be in your skull in a matter of minutes."

I look around the house as I keep the rifle aimed at him. It is getting hot in here and I am thirsty. My sister Hanna smiles at me from her photograph hung on the side wall.

Did she like to learn how to use a gun? I ask him and fight with myself not to let my tears spill on my cheeks.

"Yeah, she had fun. I remember her eyes full with light, when she hit an apple from 100 meters range. When I was explaining to her the weekly lesson, she was very enthusiastic."

"Did you have any feeling that this thing could happen?"

"I didn't like the look in her eyes."

"What do you mean?"

"I had the feeling that she was using me for a very, very bad plan. I tried to calm myself and let these feelings go, because I never had enough time for anything."

"What time did you come home?"

"I came home around 9 am. She opened the door and without even a greeting, she asked me where I was last night. I told her I was on duty, but she didn't believe me. She accused me of sleeping with the waitress. Because I became angry, I lied to her and answered her yes. I was with my waitress last night,

I replied. Then she went upstairs, and then I went outside and started to wash my van. Fifteen minutes later I heard one single bang. I thought that a tire blew out or someone hit our door with a piece of rock. When I went upstairs, I saw Hanna with the AK47 lying beside her. Her eyes were still open and a line of blood was dripping slowly from her body onto the bed. I realized that the worse had happened. Then I called you right away."

"Do you feel guilty for killing your own wife?"

"I keep telling you I didn't kill my wife."

"You shouldn't have had a gun in your house."

"That is not the point. Two years ago, she wanted to kill herself by drowning in the sea."

"Were you cheating on her all the time?"

"That is not a reason to commit suicide. I think she had a mental disorder."

"It's too late to realize that. Do you feel guilty that you realized too late and knew too little about her so called mental disorder?"

"Arber. Listen to me. I am not guilty."

"What's your last wish?"

"I don't deserve to die. Who is going to take care of my kids, if I die, you?"

"Close your eyes. Turn around and put your hands down."

Roland Shtylla closes his eyes, turns around and puts his hands down. I squeeze the trigger. Nine rounds go straight over his head ricocheting off the wall. He falls down slowly, untouched, sobbing like a child. I watch him falling and look at myself in the mirror. I don't really know what made my hand shake. I had never killed before, not even a fly. Is that why I can't kill him now? Or, maybe I knew that he was right. That is what her eyes are saying to me from the picture hung on the wall. He is not the guilty one.

I throw away the gun and vomit. Roland continues to sob and kisses my feet. I push him away and choke on my feelings. I get the hell out of there and stand outside gulping in the fresh air.

# A Fistful of Dirt

Muharrem Demi could not die. He had been lying on his bed with his eyes staring at the ceiling and refused to speak to anyone. The doctor gave no hope for his recovery. Muharrem had refused to eat and his ribs jutted out visibly on his chest. His hair had become white and wrinkles were showing on his forehead.

The pneumonia which he had persistently suffered from as a child had reappeared and racked his body. His lungs suffered from years of smoking had almost collapsed. He had now been on what was supposed to have been his deathbed for the last six months since his first heart attack. But death seemed to elude him.

Muharrem's family was tiring of this waiting around his sick bed. They had stayed close since his first heart attack, which had happened while he was taking a bath. He fell in the bathtub as it filled with hot water and he was lucky that his wife Mejreme was nearby and heard him fall. The old couple had been living alone in their big five-room house since the day their only son left for America.

That was one of the reasons for Muharrem Demi's pain. His son was living far away and did not call his aging parents often. Muharrem missed him, but said nothing ill about his son. He made excuses for his son when asked why Zylyftar Demi was "too busy" to keep in touch with his parents. Now as he lay on his deathbed, he worried that he would never see his son again. He became listless and would not eat.

Mejreme hid her tears from him so he wouldn't know how she was suffering. She coaxed him to eat, brought his medicines, but in spite of everything his health kept deteriorating. The doctors at the Emergency Department of Tirana Military Hospital had given up hope for his recovery and had suggested he go home to die, rather than go back and forth to the hospital. Then Muharrem stopped taking the prescription drugs and drank only green tea. He had asked that his burial clothes—his black suit, a white nylon shirt, a pair of blue socks and a pair of new brown shoes be kept ready in a drawer.

Then on Sunday morning Zylyftar Demi called his parents. His mother's voice over the line sounded as if she were shivering, and it sent a shiver down his spine and he felt anxiety bite at his heart. His father was not able to talk said his mother, because he was "not feeling well." But as she was ending the call with her son, Muharrem Demi turned his head toward his wife and asked for the phone.

"Death has forgotten about me, my son," the old man said in a hoarse voice. "I want you to come here." With that he passed out. The phone fell from his hand on to the floor. Zylyftar knew something was gravely wrong with his father. The line had dropped, but his father's last words were still ringing in his ears and thudding against his heart. He had planned to visit them back home a long time ago, but kept postponing it for various reasons. It never seemed the right time to spend all that money to go all that way. Now he realized his father might die and he would be thousands of miles away unable to help. He put the phone down and sat in front of the TV, without seeing anything.

The feeling of unease built up through the night and Zylyftar could not sleep. At midnight he realized it would be 6 o'clock in the morning in Albania. That was the time his mother used to wake up and make Turkish coffee boiled in a pan on the stove for his father. Zylyftar dialed his parents' phone number again. This time his father answered the phone as if he were expecting his call.

"Hello?"

"Hello, it's me, Father," he answered and felt his voice trembling.

"Hello, my son. Did you not sleep as yet?"

"Not yet."

"Isn't it midnight over there now?" the old man asked him. His voice sounded like a whisper.

"Yeah, it's just past midnight, but I was worried about you. What did you mean? Do you really want me to come? If you say "come", I will take the next plane and tomorrow I will be there."

"I am on the edge of life, but cannot go beyond. I have something that has to be done before I can go peacefully," the old man said.

Zylyftar heard his mother's voice telling the old man not to say anything and the old man replied "Be quiet, I know what I am doing." Straining to hear their voices, his eyes filled with tears and he bit his lip trying to stay in control. He felt their absence from his life so deeply in that moment that he felt he was going to burst with longing. It was a big mistake to leave his aging parents behind.

"Death will not take me away yet," he heard his father's faint voice again over the line. "Till I can be buried in the soil of Chameria, my son, I cannot die. You must go to the north of Greece, straight to the town of Paramithi and bring me a fistful of dirt from Chameria, son. You have to go. It is the only way out of this life for me. I must be buried with the soil of my hometown or I will not pass over.

"Dig the land in front of the house where I used to live, the house in which I was born and my family owned, still own for it is our ancestral property. Take a fistful of dirt from that soil and bring it back to Albania. I'll take my last breath when I see that you have really brought it to me. Do you understand, my son? I want that fistful of dirt to be buried with me or thrown on my grave," the old man said. He began gasping for breath and coughing violently.

Zylyftar Demi was silent. What was his father asking him to do? It was not easy. But how could he refuse him anything. He knew how much his father pined for his homeland.

"I know you do not feel good about it, but I have to speak the truth," his father's voice was even fainter and he had to strain to hear him. "This is all that I want from you. It will help me and everyone here as well. Your mother has not slept well for three months, since the day I fell ill. She keeps a watch on me, and is scared that I am going to die any day. But death does not come. I have even laid out my burial clothes. We called all our relatives three times to come and say their last farewell, but death will not take me."

Muharrem Demi seemed to be pleading with his son.

"Dad, you do not have to say it again. What you have asked for, consider it done. Inshallah, with God's will I'll buy a ticket and leave right away. I think I must come there first and see you, then afterwards I can go to Greece and bring that fistful of dirt for you. I don't want to waste more time. I am coming to you, Dad. We'll talk later when I get there. I will hug both of you and hold you close."

The words tumbled from Zylyftar's lips. He was now eager to set off.

"If you don't want to waste time, go straight to Chameria. I will be here waiting for you. Death will not take me away, before you come. But you must get the soil of my country and come here."

It was his mother's turn to talk to him. She made kissing sounds first and was eager to just hear his voice.

"Come here first, son, then we see. Don't listen to this crazy man. No one knows what is going to happen to you, if you go there to that country. The Greek police might catch you and put you in jail, as soon as you tell them that you are a Cham."

His mother's voice whispered her fears, "I have heard that some Chams who went back to the town of Paramithi were caught by the police and questioned and told to leave immediately, otherwise they would be jailed."

"Mom, I am an American citizen now. I have an American passport. The Greek government may treat Albanians like that, but with Americans it is different. The Greeks cannot fool around with Americans. If they stop me, I'll show them my American passport, so they will not dare to touch even a single hair on my head. I'll be just one more American tourist in that area, that's all. Don't worry. I'll go there for an hour or so not more, long enough to do my father's bidding, and I'll come home soon afterwards."

"All the Chams who went there to see their hometown were American citizens and all were humiliated by the Greek police. Albanian Chams cannot get past the border. If you really must go there, then I warn you to be very careful," his mother sounded very worried.

"I won't stay long. Just long enough to pick up some soil from Chameria. I have to go now. I have to make arrangements for this trip," he said to his mother.

"Be safe, my son. I am going to be there with you in spirit. I'll not sleep until you come here," his mother almost moaned with worry.

Zylyftar was in a dilemma. Should he listen to his father or his mother? His father was close to death. He might not live to see him. But his mother's fears were real too. What would happen if the Greek police caught him? He would not be able to grant his father's final wish nor perhaps be released in time to see him. Yet he had lived in America so long he felt more like an American than an Albanian and was certainly more American than Cham. And it seemed impossible to him that an American citizen would be arrested by the Greek police simply for visiting the village where his parents used to live.

After he had hung up, Zylyftar thought about the strange request made by his father in these last days of his life. It spoke of his desire to be buried in his hometown, his desire to go home, where the remains of his ancestors were laid to rest.

Zylyftar knew well the history of his father's people. He grew up hearing how the entire ethnic minority community was hounded out off Chameria by Greek militants led by Napoleon Zervas. Greece did not recognize the rights of its minorities. The genocide against the Chams claimed the lives of over seven thousand people and left more than two hundred thousand people homeless.

Zylyftar was ten years old when his father began telling him the story of his people, where he came from and why his family lived where they lived instead of on their ancestral land. His father showed him old pictures, treasured memories of a time when life was good for them, before they were chased from their homes. The bones of the men, women and children who were killed in the genocide litter the mountains between Greece and Albania, his father had said many times.

"I was a ten-year-old boy, the same age that you are now," his father had said to him then, "when I escaped from that town, which has now turned into a hell, haunted by the spirits of those who will never rest for the injustice done to them. My mother was holding my six-month-old sister Merushe in her arms. My poor father Abedin was the leader of a group of five Albanian families who were trying to escape from the Greek andartes. The Albanian villagers were running for their lives down the mountain. The stream of refugees was so long, no one was able to say where it ended. All of a sudden we heard gunfire coming from all directions. The Greek andartes had us under siege and most of us could not escape the ambush. I saw my mother fall on the ground lifeless," here his father would pause, fighting for control, then he would go on. "A stray bullet hit my father in the chest. He didn't die right away. Even today I can't explain where my father found the strength to scream at me, warning me to run as fast as I could and hide somewhere. The whole world seemed to be on fire. Our village was sunk in blood and clouds of smoke. My vision was dark and I didn't know where I was. I don't exactly remember how many hours had passed, when I found myself on top of a mule, which another boy my age was pulling with a rope. It took us three days to cross the border to Albania. We almost died from hunger," his father's voice would fade at the memory.

Zylyftar closed his eyes reliving his father's telling of the story of his people. He knew what he must do. For his father's sake if for no other reason. He got up and began to pack.

The taxi driver pointed to the row of houses nestled against a backdrop of surrounding hills and dark olive trees. Zylyftar could feel the emotions rolling into his throat. He had taken an eleven-hour flight to Athens and from the airport he had hired a taxi to take him north to the village where his father was born. He planned to stay only as long as it would take him to accomplish his mission. As long as it would take him to get a fistful of dirt into a plastic bag and head off to Albania.

The taxi entered a town and Zylyftar watched keenly through the taxi window with eyes already filled with tears. He was seeing it through his father's eyes. The town of Paramithi was built on the side of a hill. Even though it was the first time he was visiting it, he felt a strange affinity to the place. The crowns of the olive trees dotted the surrounding hills, birds were chirping in the otherwise silence hovering over the town. The old houses that had survived the raids years ago looked stubbornly resilient against the test of time. He could almost hear the echoes of a past life when those homes were occupied by Albanian families. Zylyftar shook his head trying to get rid of thoughts of a past that was no more. He must be imagining those echoes, it was probably the sound of the waves on the seashore far below.

Zylyftar ordered the driver to wait for him at a coffee shop and he walked through the narrow streets, with his suitcase in his hand. He knew where he was going, but still stopped in front of every single house in that row of old houses. The Albanian homes were one-storey or two-storeys high, built solidly with stone a long time ago. Some of the homes had been turned into museums. Some had been abandoned and bolted since the day when their Albanian inhabitants had been expelled from them. Those who survived hid in the mountains, waiting to cross the border into Albania. Some of the houses had been taken over by Greeks or Vlachs who lived there. This news had filtered through to the Cham refugees, like Zylyftar's father, who had escaped to settle in Albania. They longed for news of their hometown and eagerly devoured every scrap of news and then just as eagerly circulated it further.

At last, he came to the home which belonged to the Demi family. It stood silent. He knew it from his father's detailed description of it. Also from the basketball court that had been built close to it. Zylyftar felt a shiver run up his spine. The court was a recent addition and he had read on Albanian forums on the Internet that the court had been built over a shallow incline which had been used as a mass grave for hundreds of missing ethnic Albanians.

Zylyftar held his breath as he stood in front of his grandparents' home. It was midday and the heat of the sun added to the heat of his apprehension. He checked the area around the house and did not see anybody. He opened his suitcase and from a bottom compartment took out a little scoop and a plastic bag. He entered the front yard of the house and began to dig the ground with the little scoop. He filled the plastic bag with the dirt, placed it in the suitcase with a sigh of relief at having completed his mission.

The suitcase felt unusually heavy. He had to hold it across his chest with both arms. That fistful of dirt was more valuable than a fistful of gold. For his father, it was a piece of his country, his ancestral home, a tangible part of his memories.

"I will not come back here," he said aloud to himself, "so I should record this place for my father and myself." He took out his small video camera and started to record the house, going around to the sides and then focused on the little hole where the little scoop was still stuck in the soil. He left the camera facing the hole and stood before it, recording himself.

He bent and put his lips to the ground, kissing the land of his ancestors.

As he was preparing to leave, out of the corner of his eye he saw a shadow moving behind the curtains of the front window. He pretended he hadn't seen anyone, but heard some footsteps approaching him. He turned around and saw a woman. She looked Greek and she looked angry and scared at the same time.

"Kalla ise?" she asked him in Greek.

"Kalla," he answered her. "And you?" he asked in English. "I'm sorry I don't speak Greek at all; my parents lived here over 50 years ago."

The woman came closer to him.

"I saw you taking pictures of my house," she accused him.

"Yes, I was taking some pictures. Pictures of my father's family home. This house is not yours. You have it for use. You don't own it. All the homes in this town belonged to Albanians. I came here to take back pictures and a bit of soil from this house for my father to see. He is ill and may die at any moment."

"Are you a Cham?"

"Yes, I am Cham."

"Get the hell out from here, otherwise I am going to call the police," the woman was suddenly aggressive.

"I came here today to get a fistful of dirt from the land that belongs to my father, to throw on his grave when he dies. Now I have got it, I am leaving."

With that Zylyftar turned to leave, but his feet would not move. The land seemed to be holding him there.

"If I leave now and take only this handful of dirt to my father, his will is not fulfilled. The land is still occupied," he thought.

He left and went back towards the cab. As he reached it a police car appeared and stopped in front of him. A policeman got out and came up to him speaking in Greek. He heard the word "karta." He understood that he had to show the policeman his identification papers. He took out his American passport. The policeman spoke to him this time in English.

"Excuse me, Sir, but were you trespassing at that house over there?"

"No sir. I was not trespassing. That is my home. A long time ago it was taken by force from my father's family. It is still legally my home."

"Do you live there?"

"No, sir. I don't live there now. I live in America."

"Then you were trespassing," the policeman insisted. There was silence for a moment. "Are you an American citizen?" He looked doubtfully at Zylyftar's passport.

"Yes, sir, I am an American. My grandparents lived in that house. Your government kicked us out from there and killed those who weren't able to escape."

Zylyftar spoke boldly to the policeman looking him straight in the eye.

The policeman took his gun out and raised it till the muzzle touched Zylyftar's forehead. The cold metal of the gun made him shiver.

"Your name sounds like a Muslim name. Are you an Albanian?"

"Yes, I am of Albanian descent. I am Cham."

"Oh, Cham? Ahh. So you came here to join Chameria region with Albania, right?"

"No sir, I came here to see my father's home."

Anger and hatred seemed to flare in the eyes of the policeman.

"All of you should be killed for good. You are traitors. You Chams collaborated with the German Nazis during their occupation of Greece, so you have no right to come back and call this "home." You are German "Schumannschaft," minority traitors who fight local people all over Europe. You are traitors." The policeman almost spat the last words, still holding the gun to Zylyftar's head.

"You don't know your history, my friend," said Zylyftar defiantly. "There were groups made up of Albanian Chams who fought for the liberation of Greece as well. There were more Cham patriots fighting for their country than the few Chams who collaborated with the Nazis."

Zylyftar could not stop. Even if it got him into trouble he had to say what was right.

"The ethnic cleansing of a whole minority cannot be justified by this stupid ignorant twisting of facts. You are pointing a gun at me, an American citizen, who is visiting this country. I am going to call the Embassy and tell them that the Greek police are threatening me."

The policeman's hand waivered, but he kept the muzzle of his gun against Zylyftar's forehead.

"What do you have in your suitcase?"

"I have my clothes and some dirt."

"What?"

"Dirt! Soil from my father's ancestral land."

"Are you out of your mind? You are crazy. What do you need the dirt for?"

"To throw it on my father's grave, when he dies."

"What for? You guys don't have enough dirt in Albania?"

"No, he wants to be buried with soil from Chameria."

"Come with me to the police station."

"What for?"

"You are accused of trespassing and stealing property. Move."

"Let me pay the taxi driver first," said Zylyftar. He took out his wallet pulled out a few Euros and tossed it toward the taxi driver, who grabbed at it. He bowed to get into the police car and the policeman hit him hard on the back of his head with the revolver. Everything became dark as he lost unconscious.

Zylyftar Demi did not know where he was. His vision was foggy and a heavy smoke seemed to be rising from the ground. His suitcase lay beside him. He could swear he heard voices coming from the suitcase. He reached out and lifted the lid of the suitcase and then dropped it immediately, crouching away from it terrified. He wiped at his eyes and looked again at the suitcase. It was opening. A pair of disembodied hands crawled out of the suitcase feeling their way around as though looking for something, then retraced their steps and disappeared back into the case again.

"Who are you?" he asked tremulously.

"I am your grandfather!" said a voice from the suitcase.

"I am your great grandfather!" Another voice said.

"I am the voice of your ancestors!" a deeper third voice whispered.

Zylyftar closed his eyes and when he opened it he realized he was in a jail with about thirty other people standing or sitting around, whom he suspected were Albanians like himself. They too must have been arrested as suspected spies. His vision was blurring again and he wiped his eyes and realized there was blood on his face. He tried to get up from the floor which was covered with plastic sheets, but could barely raise himself up as he felt pain all over his body. An old man with a deeply wrinkled face came towards him.

"They beat you up really badly," the old man said. "They kicked you, they stepped on you with their shoes, they smashed your head on the wall, they spit on your face. They ripped up your passport."

He took out some pages he had ripped from Zylyftar's American passport which he had quietly snatched off the ground where they had been thrown. Zylyftar tried to get to his feet again, but his knees were very weak. A young man was screaming through the only window of the cell, begging in Albanian for water. The word uje was repeated several times by most of the prisoners. Zylyftar was thirsty as well. More than six hours had passed in the cell and his throat was dry. Another hour passed before a policeman attacked the prisoners with a fire hose. The men fell on top of each other with the force of the water.

Zylyftar looked around for his suitcase which seemed to have disappeared, but could not see it anywhere. He shivered to the roots of his hair as he imagined his father's disappointment. In frustration he hit the wall very hard with his fist bruising it severely. There was chaos in the cell and everyone seemed to be shouting. He was beginning to lose hope when a policeman appeared at the window and ordered the prisoners to calm down and they would get out from there one at a time.

Finally, Zylyftar was led to a main hall where three policemen sat interviewing prisoners. Some of the prisoners were being beaten. His turn before the panel came quickly. A policeman raised Zylyftar's suitcase and placed it on top of the table and opened it. The policeman pointed to the plastic bag holding the soil.

"We thought you hid drugs in there. Take it," he shouted and threw the bag at Zylyftar who was startled and unable to grab it before it fell to the floor.

"This guy must be a madman," the policeman who had arrested him laughed, pointing at him. "He carries dirt around with him. Better to let him go."

"This detention is illegal. You have no right to do this," Zylyftar spoke boldly. The first policeman hit him on the side of his head with a wooden baton. He felt a searing pain shoot through his head and blood spouted from a gash on his cheekbone.

"You go back to your village to steal more dirt and you'll see what will happen to you, asshole," the policeman yelled at him, laughing hysterically.

Zylyftar clutched the plastic bag hiding it against his body. A few hours later he was on a bus along with the other prisoners headed toward the Albanian border.

The door to the old Tirana house where he grew up was wide open. Zylyftar got out of the cab, bedraggled and filthy from his long journey and ordeal in jail. He stood in front of his old home. There were people, mostly men, dressed in black talking to each other in the front yard. The men were smoking and drinking boiled coffee. The women looked sorrowful as if in mourning and were assisting in serving others.

Zylyftar's heart was heavy. Fear clutched at his throat. His father—they had come to see his father. He shivered and ran toward the house. The guests did not recognize him. They were shocked at the state of his clothes and the wounds visible on his face. But one person recognized him immediately.

As soon as he entered the front yard his mother cried out, raising her hands towards the sky in thanksgiving and ran to him. She hugged him close, desperately, as though afraid that he could leave again. Zylyftar pulled her along with him into the house looking for his father. His heart was so full he could not speak, but his eyes feverishly fixed on the bed positioned in the middle of the room, where his father lay with his eyes open, breathing heavily. The room was filled with the sound of his labored breathing.

Zylyftar had one arm around his mother and in the other hand he held the plastic bag. He bent close to his father and pressed the bag into the feeble hand lying on the bed.

"Here is the Chameria soil you asked for, Father," Zylyftar said bringing his father's hand with the bag pressed against it up before his eyes. The dirt was black and dry inside the bag. "This dirt comes from Chameria, Father, from your home in Chameria." His voice choked on the emotions that coursed through him and he laid his head on the pillow beside his father's head.

Muharrem Demi's eyes moved to the bag, his facial muscles struggled and then broke into a faint smile. Slowly it seemed life was coming back into his feeble body. He had barely spoken since his son's call. Everyone had given up hope of him lasting much longer.

Now he moved his head so he could see his son's face as they lay side by side on the pillow. Tears slipped from his eyes and he began to sob. He touched his head to his son's and blinked his eyes in gratitude. His fingers seemed to grow stronger as they clutched the bag and tried to reach inside. Zylyftar opened the bag and his father's weak fingers reached into the dirt, grabbing desperately at the soil. He sighed deeply, his soul seeming to stretch on the sigh of peace. Emotions of pain and longing flitted across his face, the memories flooding in and lying at rest.

"God bless you, my son" the old man's voice was barely audible. "God bless you," he repeated once again, "for this that you have done. I have my Chameria with me now."

Muharrem looked towards his wife, "Bring some raki. We must celebrate. Our son is home again."

Mejreme's eyes were filled with tears, but she laughed with a relief that came like peace settling in her soul. Yes, their son was home. But most importantly he had lifted the curse of exile from her husband's life and it would be extended to affect all their lives.

For Muharrem, if death came now it would be the final liberation. There would be peace in this home now.

# The Talking Clocks

Barbara McKay couldn't sleep since the day that Indrit Farka had been found dead. That was thirteen days ago, and she had since been dreaming of wealth and prosperity in these long hours of wakefulness.

Barbara could not believe that Indrit, her mysterious former husband, was dead. As his widow, she had been handed the keys to his apartment. She could hardly wait to enter it and search inside for the golden coins that she knew he had a habit of buying and collecting during his short life of prosperity. Having not even seen them yet, she was already blinded by the dazzling prospect of golden coins. Those coins could be anywhere and everywhere, on the dusty shelves, under the wooden floorboards, in the oven which he never used, under the sink or the mattress. Her raving fancies even led her to suspect that the dust covering the cold walls and sparse furniture of his apartment might be gold dust.

Excitement consumed her and she could think of nothing else but the prospect of opening the door to untold wealth with this key that she gripped constantly in the palm of her hand, unable to put down lest it somehow disappear.

"I hope he has left everything to me. I could say "goodbye" to all my problems," muttered Barbara for the hundredth time since she had heard the news.

The very thought of her ex-husband however made her shiver with revulsion. She shook off uneasiness as she parked slowly by the sidewalk in front of the small block of apartments. She got out of the car and walked to the front entrance of the building, remembering the last time she had left not expecting to return ever again.

She let herself into the building's tiny darkened foyer and walked down the grimy corridor to the back of the building where Indrit Farka lived in one of the two apartments located there.

As she turned the key in the lock to get in, her mind flashed back to her first date with Indrit Farka. They had met for the first time in a seedy nightclub in Toronto. He asked her to dance and after that first dance Indrit surprised her with a proposal of marriage. He offered her five thousand dollars if she would marry him. It would be a fake marriage on paper only, he promised. Only for a year and after that both of them would go their separate lives like nothing happened.

It was done. Barbara had pocketed the money and Indrit got the marriage certificate in his mailbox. They saw each other a couple more times, after she became "the bride."

Indrit Farka was an Albanian immigrant who had entered Canada illegally and continued to stay, working at illegal jobs for cash. He had found a job as a mechanic and his plan was to get his legal status papers and then go back to his country to get married to an Albanian woman. The years passed and they lived separate lives. Barbara spent all of the money during the first three months following their marriage.

In the year that followed, Indrit tried a couple of times to get in touch with her. On one occasion he asked her to live with him, like a real wedded couple, because he thought someone was checking up on his legal immigration status. During one of these stay overs they had sex and Barbara found herself pregnant. She gave birth to a baby boy, whom she named

Jeffrey, after her father. But Indrit and she still continued to live separately. The arrangement suited them. Indrit was easy to get along with. He recognized Jeffrey as his son and had paid child support always on time, until this last month when no cheque had arrived and he had been found dead in his apartment.

Barbara opened the door of his apartment and put the keys in her pocket. The door creaked open, sounding like a groan. A faint stench of death mixed with strong disinfectants hit her in the face as she entered. She remembered that Indrit had been found dead by a neighbor several days after he had died. She shivered with uneasiness then nearly collapsed in fright when his voice sounded through the heavy air.

"Good evening! It is 5 p.m."

It was Indrit Farka's voice with a metallic ring to it coming from a Braille Quartz Clock on the wall. Barbara shivered violently. She remembered that he had this strange fascination with clocks that recorded greetings in a human voice and called them out with the time. She never really understood why her former husband had this weird fetish of recording his voice on clocks. Once she had questioned him about the talking clocks and he had replied that he was lonely, that the house was quiet and the clocks filled his home with human voices.

Suddenly another clock chimed loudly and a message floated eerily through the stifling room to her ears.

"I bought this clock to remind you that I love you even beyond death."

Barbara spun around looking to see if the voice had come from the same clock. Fear crawled up her spine. She began to think that it was a mistake to come alone to his apartment. But she had to search it herself before she brought anyone else in here. She did not want to stir up more claims to ownership or have anyone question her right to Indrit's possessions. She had to find the hidden diamonds and golden rings she knew Indrit used to buy with his earnings.

Indrit had once told her that he was putting his money into gold and diamonds as an investment. He did not trust the banks. She knew he used to work as a mechanic in an auto garage seven days a week. He lived alone and had no addictive expensive habits like alcohol or smoking. When he was lonely he used to call Barbara. But of late she had not been answering him. She was seeing someone else and had recently moved into her boyfriend's home. That was why when the police contacted her to tell her that her husband was dead, she had said it was a wrong number, till the officer mentioned her husband as Indrit Farka.

Barbara shook her head trying to get rid of the uneasy feeling that was now centered on the back of her neck. It felt like she was being watched. Like the clocks ticking on every wall turned their faces to look at her.

She left the house quickly and went to her car and opened the trunk. She got a tool kit which she had packed with a hammer, shovel, screwdriver, pliers and a hand saw. She entered the apartment again and looked around very carefully. Where should she look first?

"I better think like him. If I want to hide something in my house, which place would be the best, so no one would find it? If I were him, I would hide the gold under the wooden floor. No one could think that they were walking on gold. I better look for loose floor boards," she spoke aloud.

She found reassurance in the sound of her own voice and went to work on a loose floor board. She took the hammer and smashed it on the floor. She heard a dry bang. The hammer did not do any serious damage. She hit the floor again and used a lever, to open the crack in the wood. She was engrossed in loosening the wooden floorboard when the sound of a human voice came from the direction of the bedroom.

"It is now 5.15 p.m." It was clearly Indrit's thick accented voice. A layer of cold sweat broke out on Barbara's forehead.

"Leave me alone!" she screamed and looked with anger and desperation toward the room where the voice had come from. She wiped the sweat off her brow and closed her eyes for a moment.

"What the hell is wrong with you? Why did you record your voice in all these clocks?" she yelled aloud, but no one answered from the empty rooms.

A faint movement of air blew a lock of her hair across her face. She swung around startled, flailing her arms in defense. The kitchen window was slightly open and the netting had been ripped. That must have been the window that one of the neighbors used to get in to investigate the foul smell coming out of the apartment. The police had said that the neighbor had cut the net with a pocket knife and found Indrit Farka still lying on his couch and the TV was on. Indrit had been holding the remote controller in his left hand and his eyes were half open. The neighbor had dialed 911 and when the paramedics arrived they took his body to the morgue. They said that Indrit had been dead for two weeks.

A deep booming chime sounded from the bedroom. This time there were echoing chimes from other clocks on the walls of the hallway and the living area as well. It sounded like the chimes and then his voice were coming at her from all directions.

"Good evening, it is 5.30 p.m.," came from one clock. Then the other clocks picked it up in an eerie echo effect.

"I will follow you everywhere. I will be with you wherever you go." His voice echoed through the rooms and swirled around her. It was as if he were flying around her head, speaking from behind her. When she swung around the sound was still behind her.

"I will chase you, chase you, chase you..." Then "Why did you leave me, leave me, leave me..." The echoes spun around her making her dizzy. "Why did you take my son from me, from me, from me..." The voice was a whisper now "You left me alone, alone, alone..."

Barbara's head was spinning. She fell on her knees, pressing her hands to her ears to shut out the sound of his voice.

"This is crazy. This cannot be happening. He is dead. Dead and gone," she gasped out, holding tight to the hammer in her hand, ready to use it as a weapon.

As her glance went to the ceiling, her eyes narrowed on the ceiling tiles. They were uneven. Her eyes gleamed. She could move that easily. She pushed a chair towards an uneven section in the corner.

"Either I find the treasure, or I'll die trying," Barbara said out loud gritting her teeth. She began ripping the ceiling tiles apart checking to see if there was a stash of gold. But she saw nothing. The tiles fell and the gaping hole in the ceiling widened.

"It is so easy to become a bad person, but so hard to be good." Indrit Farka's voice echoed in Barbara's head. She had heard him saying this many times when they lived together. She had not agreed with him. She had told him that she would do anything to be able to take care of her son.

The clocks chimed six o'clock.

"I am tired and weak," said Indrit Farka's voice. "I can barely speak. I see you going in and out of these empty rooms. You can't believe that I am dead when my voice tells you the correct time. I may have passed on, but I am still here."

Barbara's teeth were chattering with fright. The same light wind coming through the open window seemed to be carrying the hushed words to her ear. Ghostly words like ghostly fingers caressing her ears.

"Do you remember when we used to live together? They were happy times, when we used to wake up and go to work. You used to make me hot lemon tea, which I would drink all at once till my throat burned."

"Yes," whispered Barbara stricken with horror. It was not the clocks speaking any longer. Or was it? Where was his voice coming from?

"Do you remember how you used to spread butter on my toast and put feta cheese and black olives on it, and I ate like never before.

"Then you would kiss me on my lips, as I was trying to put my clothes on and rush to the car to go to work. Do you remember, Barbara?

"We were happy together Barbara, until the day you left. You never told me why. You never came back. You would not speak to me. You would not let my son speak to me. He loved me, but you kept him away from me. Why, Barbara, why?" The words were swirling around and around her. Coming at her from all directions.

Barbara got to her feet fighting to stay calm. She tried to shake off the hallucinations. They had to be hallucinations, she insisted to herself. This could not be happening. Indrit Farka was dead and she was entitled to his money which she needed for her son. It was not a crime to look around for valuables that her son's father had left behind. She was so sure that Indrit had left something of value behind.

"Good evening, it is 7 p.m.," she heard his voice once again. This time she could not figure out where the voice was coming from. It wasn't coming from the living room or from the bedroom. It was coming from the kitchen area. She entered the kitchen slowly fearing she would be confronted by a ghost. She sighed when she saw another talking clock.

"It is 15 degrees Centigrade. It is cold. It was always cold when you were not here. I missed the warmth of humans, of your warm body. I was sad, because I missed your eyes, which were like broken mirrors. I could see myself reflected in a thousand shining pieces."

Barbara spun around, seeing nothing, then backed out into the hall. A huge clock on the wall lit up as she moved in front of it.

"Today is September 15," Indrit's voice came from the clock. Barbara looked haunted as she stared up at the clock. She knew it was October. The clock had stopped on September 15, the day of Indrit's death. But the clock's timing mechanism was still working only the date was not changing.

"You will not find anything here," the words seemed to be blowing in from the kitchen window with the torn net. "These talking clocks are the only treasures you will find here. These clocks are my link to you; they will whisper my words to you.

"There is no treasure here for you. There never was." The words whispered swirled around her, chilling her to the bone.

"Stop it! Stop it!" screamed Barbara. She kicked a kitchen cabinet door open, yanked the door off its rusty hinge and placed it over the window, trying to shut out the breeze blowing in. It was then she realized that even though the apartment was ventilated because of the open window, the stench of death and disinfectant was still overpowering. It was as if she were standing in a butcher's shop.

One of the clocks on the wall clicked and Indrit's voice flowed from it.

"There is no treasure. There never was. Come here now, come closer to this clock."

Barbara didn't know if the clock was moving towards her or she was being drawn towards it. But she found herself staring at the huge mirrored dial of a Quantum Digital Clock.

"Come closer. Put your lips to this clock and give me your breath. Your lips on my lips, my love. I am the air that you breathe, this cold air that enters your lungs and freezes you. Breathe my darling! I am in you. You will be with me. Forever. We will never be parted."

Barbara felt her throat being squeezed with invisible hands. The clocks were chiming all together. Louder and louder. They were in her head pounding against her brain. She collapsed unable to breathe. White foam frothed out of her mouth. The foam turned yellowish. Suddenly she saw the foam turn into a figure. It was Indrit Farka and he was wearing white, the same suit he wore when they got married, at their fake wedding. Real or fake, they had been married and had had a son.

Indrit was smiling and his hand was held out to her, as he had held it out to her at the courthouse before they were married.

She stretched out her hand and touched his fingers.

The last words she heard were "there was no treasure here for you to find. It is all in a trust for Jeffery. He loved me. It will be all his, only his, when it is time."

# The Chaser

I was on vacation overseas when Jerry died. He was one of my best tenants, who lived on the first floor apartment of my triplex building for more than eighteen years. Jerry used to take care of the building as if it was his own.

I felt awful that I wasn't there when he breathed his last. I returned to Canada from Albania two weeks after his death. Daniel, the tenant who lived in the top floor apartment discovered the body five days after Jerry had died. He noticed that the lights in Jerry's apartment were always on through the night, shining through the thin curtains onto the landing in front of his apartment. Also, the TV was always on. But when he knocked on the door there was no answer. Then on the fifth day he noticed a bad smell coming from under the front door and through the window which Jerry always kept slightly open when he was home in the summertime. One of Jerry's friends called several times but got no answer except for Jerry's recorded voice on the answering machine, "Hey, this is Jerry. State your business, keep it short, hang up."

Daniel and Jerry's friend went through the open window into the apartment and found Jerry lying dead on his huge couch. Daniel dialed 911.

When I got home from the airport and heard Daniel's messages on my answering machine, I immediately went to Jerry's apartment. I saw Jerry's ex-wife Fiona standing and smoking in front of his apartment with the doors wide open. At that time I had no idea that she was his ex-wife. She was in her fifties, blonde and in good shape.

As she saw me, she approached and shook my hand telling me who she was. It was then that I saw the big truck parked to the left of the building loaded with Jerry's furniture. A tall, brown-haired man came out of the apartment and joined us. He introduced himself as Brian McGill and said he was with Fiona. Brian sneezed loudly and pointed toward the truck.

"Most of his furniture and belongings are covered with dust. His stuff is too old and not worth taking with us. Fiona is insisting that we have to take them as sellable property," Brian said.

I knew that this guy used to be Jerry's best friend till he fell in love with Fiona. Jerry had told me that his wife took their son and left with Brian. Now they were here taking his possessions. I had an uneasy feeling that these two were not leaving Jerry alone even after death. But I did not want to get involved, so I did not question them.

"Do you know if he left a will?" Fiona asked me straight forward, jerking her head towards the apartment.

"I don't know," I answered.

Fiona and Brian loaded ten bags and fifteen suitcases from Jerry's apartment and then gave me the keys to the place. They got into their truck, disappearing in a cloud of black smoke coming from the exhaust. I watched until they turned on Old Dundas to get to the main road.

As I entered Jerry's apartment I still couldn't believe that he was dead. The sound of my footsteps on the wooden floor echoed through the apartment, and I waited to hear the sound of his habitual choking cough. I opened his fridge and saw there was still food in it. There was a carton of milk, a half full bottle of Heineken, prime ribs and peaches. I knew from experience that most tenants never cleaned out their apartments when they left. Jerry hadn't intended to leave.

There were spider webs hanging from the ceiling and the whole apartment smelled of dust and moisture and there was a faint smell of death hanging in the air. Daniel said they had aired out the apartment for a week and that it had been worse.

I heard a strange noise and swung around. A huge grey cat padded over to stand in front of me, looking at me in silence. Her eyes were like live coals and they fixed on my eyes like laser beams. It was Joyce, Jerry's cat, whom he had for years. She was now abandoned. Fiona had not taken her. Joyce mewed brushing against my legs with her tail. Then just as suddenly she ran through the apartment and out the open door. I wondered who would care for her.

Since then I barely ever saw the cat. Once or twice I saw it beside my neighbor's house but not often.

A year had passed since Jerry died and everything had gone back to normal fairly quickly. Then one day a strange thing happened. As I was coming back from work, I saw Jerry's cat in front of his old apartment, which was now occupied by a couple from Jamaica. Her fur looked dirty with brown patches that looked as if they had been singed by fire. The cat looked directly at me, making eye contact with the same laser-beam-like effect, and mewed several times. I didn't react but felt very uneasy. Where had Joyce been? Why was she back at Jerry's apartment? She was looking at me as though she recognized me and waved her tail high up in the air. She came closer and leaned her body against my leg and an involuntary shiver went up my spine. Then she ran off like a flash and I saw her disappear between the flowerbeds in my backyard.

I thought that I would not see her again, but two days later Joyce came to my workplace, which is an auto repair shop located more than five blocks from my home. I was changing the oil in one of the cars in the shop when I suddenly noticed Joyce rubbing against my shoes. I felt sorry for her and was surprised how she had managed to find her way to my workplace.

"What do you want, Joyce? Tell me, what do you want from me?" I asked her, looking at her big haunting eyes. She looked back at me, her eyes seeming to pierce through mine.

"Now go. Leave from here. You can't come to my work, you know? Even my wife doesn't come here. My daughter doesn't know where I work. Go. Leave now!"

But Joyce played deaf. I knew that she was smart and understood a lot, as Jerry had always told me. But she didn't want to go. She sat in front of me, watching every single move I made, making me extremely uncomfortable. When I finished work at 4 p.m., I saw Joyce sitting beside my car and I felt that strange shiver of unease again. She followed me to the driver's side door, mewing at me. This time her mews sounded angry. I opened my lunch bag and took out some chicken pieces left over from my lunch. I threw them to her and she pounced on them and started to eat hungrily. I watched her for a minute and then got into my car. As I drove off, I saw Joyce sitting and staring at my car.

As soon as I got home, I got out my phone book and looked up Sarah's phone number. Sarah lived close by and was an animal lover. She knew things about animals that were not even in books. I thought she would be able to advise me on what to do with Joyce, the strange cat of my dead tenant.

"Hello, Sarah?"

"Hi!" she answered.

"Look, I wonder if you can help me."

"Sure, what's going on?"

"I know you know a lot about animals, especially strange ones."

"What kind of strange animal?"

"It's a cat. She belonged to one of my tenants who died a year ago. No one took care of her, after Jerry passed away. His ex-wife took everything away, but didn't bother to take Joyce, his cat and she became a stray."

"Oh, that's sad," Sarah said.

"Now suddenly Joyce has appeared again and she chases me wherever I go. Once I saw her in front of my apartment. Today she came to my workplace, which is five blocks away from where I live. I don't know how this is even possible. How could she find my garage, which is far from my home?"

"Well, I think she must have followed you several times. Do you take the same road every single day?"

"Yes, I do. I drive on Dundas Street East, until I reach Bloor Street. My garage is located very close by that major intersection."

"Yeah, it's simple then, since you are going in the same direction every day, it's very easy for her to follow you."

"But how is that possible, Sarah. I don't walk I drive. She can't be following my car. She seems to be chasing me though. And her eyes are so creepy. They pierce through me like lasers."

Sarah was quiet for awhile, listening carefully to my responses to her questions.

"Why do you think she is following me?"

"She is probably feeling lonely."

"After one year? Why didn't she come find me earlier?"

"She must have stayed somewhere else. Did Jerry have anyone else who could take care of her?"

"His ex-wife took all his stuff from the apartment, but left the cat behind."

"Do you know if the cat went to the ex-wife's place?"

"I don't know about that. But then why is she coming after me?"

"You are the chosen one, because you lived in the same building where she lived before she was abandoned."

"What is that supposed to mean?"

"She is abandoned. She doesn't have a home. She wants to make a home in familiar surroundings, familiar things, familiar people. That could now be you. She wants to be close to her master."

"Are you kidding me?"

"No, not at all."

"This is fucking crazy!"

"From what you have told me, yes, it is not a normal situation. And I warn you to be careful, Cesar. Do not attempt to hurt this animal."

"This is ridiculous!" I laughed at her. "You are freaking me out more than that damned cat. I better call the animal control people, even if they laugh at me for being spooked by a cat. If they don't help then I better buy a gun."

"I am not saying that you have to take any action like that. But be aware of the consequences, if you don't let her in."

"What consequences?"

"Just be careful of Joyce. She is normal now, but still there is something about this story that makes me very afraid for you. Don't piss her off by trying to harm her."

"That's bullshit. I am the one who is pissed already."

"Cesar, I'm trying to understand your situation there. If you don't like what I said, just forget about it. I am not the best animal expert here," Sarah said and hung up on me. I had the feeling she did not want to be involved in this case.

I sat silently for a moment and didn't know what to do. It was hard to stay calm. There was no way that I could bring Joyce back into my building. My wife didn't like pets and neither did I. My hands were shaking as I went through the Yellow Pages looking for the phone numbers of animal shelters. I took a piece of paper and a pen and wrote down a list of them.

An hour later, I hung up on the last number. Nobody wanted to take the cat. Everybody had a solution that did not involve them taking the cat, but instead involved my keeping it.

Are you the owner, sir?

Is something wrong with the cat?

Is she wounded? Where is she now?

Oh, we can't do anything, sir. If she is hurt or sick, then we can take her to our shelter.

If that was her home, then it would be better if you offer her shelter.

I was fuming. What did they mean by "her home?" This was not her home for God's sake. This is my home, my building and I decide who is to be my guest, who is to stay here. I put the matter of the cat out of my mind and went to bed.

I had an uneasy sleep. I was rolling around in my bed with my eyes closed, but my mind would not rest. Suddenly I heard someone banging hard on the front door. I got up and ran downstairs to see who was there. What I saw had me gasping with terror. Joyce stood there in the shape of a human, standing on her back paws. Her teeth were longer and feral, sticking menacingly out of her jaws. I slammed the door shut and ran upstairs, shut and bolted the bedroom door. I was shaking so hard that I woke up. I could feel sweat beading my forehead as I opened my eyes and looked around. I was still in my bed. It was a dream, a nightmare. I should have felt relieved, but my heart was still pounding like never before. I could not go back to sleep and could hardly wait till morning to call Sarah.

"I'm sorry Sarah, but I couldn't sleep. I see her now in my dreams," I whispered.

"Why are you whispering, Cesar?" Sarah asked.

"This is not a joke. Why is she coming after me?"

"I told you, she is feeling abandoned."

It occurred to me that Sarah did not ask who I was talking about. She seemed to have expected me to call back about Joyce.

"Don't you think this is abnormal behavior for a cat?"

"This is not a normal cat, Cesar. I told you that yesterday. From what you tell me she is a chaser. She has a mission. And it involves you now."

"What does it mean, Sarah? This sounds dangerous. I think Jerry wants me to have her. Dead Jerry. But I can't take her. Jerry knew my wife and I don't like animals. My wife will kill me if I bring a cat into our home."

"How are you going to get rid of her? Do you want to kill her? Cats have many lives. And this cat, this chaser, is not easily destroyed."

"What should I do?"

"If I were you, I'd find the ex-wife and ask her to take it." Sarah hung up. This time I really knew that she didn't want to have anything more to do with this issue.

I went to work in a very bad mood. As I was changing a tire, my partner Andrew came up to me with a cigarette in his hand. He didn't speak to me, but touched me slightly on the shoulder. I turned my head towards him but my eyes caught on the cat that was standing behind him. It was her—Joyce. It was the second time that she had come to my garage.

"I am going to kill this bitch," I exploded and ran toward her with a big hammer in my hand, but Joyce disappeared in the woods behind the garage. I came back to the garage, shaking with nerves.

"Do you want to go to jail for killing an animal?" Andrew said to me. I saw him go out in the direction in which Joyce had disappeared beckoning her by making a smacking sound with his lips. That day Andrew left early taking Joyce with him in his car. I saw the cat curled up in the back windshield, staring straight at me all the way out of sight. I felt relieved, but still very uneasy. I had a feeling that the relief was going to be short-lived.

The next day Joyce escaped from Andrew's house and came back to my building. I saw her sitting on the edge of the backyard watching me with those evil laser-beam eyes. I tried to shoo her away as I was getting in my car. She didn't move an inch. What the heck was happening? Why was she chasing me? Was it some kind of unfinished business on Jerry's part? I didn't believe in life after death, but how else could I explain this strange cat's strange behavior.

I didn't want her. My family didn't want her but the cat kept coming around me and my building, my workplace, reminding me of Jerry. The cat must miss her dead master. When he was alive, I visited him more often than anyone else. Jerry used to care for the main areas of my building like it was his own. I used to talk to him anytime I saw him in front of his door or in the corridors of the building. Maybe that was it. The cat wanted to replace her dead master with a master who was a real friend to Jerry. I decided to take Sarah's advice and track down the ex-wife and tell her to take the cat. If she could take Jerry's possessions without anyone's permission, then the cat was one of his possessions and she should take it.

That evening I managed to get Fiona's phone number from Jerry's file in my office. I called right away.

The phone rang and rang, and as I was going to put it down, it was answered.

"Hello?"

"Hello, I am Fiona's ex-husband's landlord. I need to talk to her."

There was a pause.

"This is Matt McGill. Fiona's boyfriend Brian was my brother."

"Can I speak to one of them?" Again there was silence. "I need to discuss something urgent with Fiona or Brian."

"Fiona and Brian were killed a month ago in a freak accident," Matt McGill said.

My heart started to throb painfully in my throat.

"What freak accident?" I barely got the words out.

"There was a fire in the annex to this house. Just in their part of the house. They died in their sleep from smoke inhalation, but the son was alright. Most of their stuff was destroyed in the flat. Weirdest thing you ever saw. Some pieces of furniture were burned to a cinder and some furniture beside it was just fine. Freakish if you ask me," Matt sounded unnerved. "Who did you say you were?"

"Never mind," I said. Or think I said the words. I just slammed the phone down and ran into the bedroom and sat in the closet for an hour before I calmed down enough to realize where I was.

I went outside and looked around the front yard of the building. Joyce was sitting in the yard, stock still, staring at me. I approached her slowly, pretending to be friendly. I had enough. She couldn't fuck around with me. No one could play crazy games with me like this.

She was making me angry. Dangerously angry.

I looked around to see if anybody was in sight. Varsity Road was quiet. It had begun to rain. I closed my eyes and kicked her as hard as I could. I saw her body fly through the air. I watched her fall to the ground. She didn't move. I walked closer to her body. I kicked her again with the tip of my steel-toed boot. Joyce didn't give any sign that she was alive. I turned away and walked back to the building. I stopped in front of the main entrance and took my keys from my pocket.

I turned and looked toward her once more to make sure she had not moved. My eyes widened in terror. She was not there in the spot where she had landed when I had kicked her. Suddenly I felt sharp spikes biting into the back of my neck. I tried to reach behind to grab whatever it was that was sucking the life out of me. It was Joyce! We struggled as I thrashed about trying to dislodge her feral teeth. She would not let go. My sight started to darken, fade away. I couldn't breathe.

Since then I only saw Joyce once. It was the second anniversary of Jerry's death. I saw Joyce peeing on my grave. As soon as she finished urinating, Joyce ran toward a tomcat waiting for her at the side of the road. The tomcat gave a choking cough and then wiped its paw across its nose and mouth. I remember Jerry used to do that.

# Beyond the Edge

It was early in the morning and gunshots already echoed off the surrounding buildings followed by the acrid smell of gunpowder. An empty shell ricocheted off a wall hitting the window and cracking the glass before landing on the balcony floor of the Army Hotel room in Shkodër, in northwestern Albania.

Geraldina Hazizllari jerked backwards, her heart pounding. She had been standing inches away from the cracked glass. She glanced back into the room which she shared with her husband Arben and their two-year-old son. She moved the curtain aside and peered out the window again.

A throng of about a hundred people; men, women and children were marching down the main road, some holding guns in their hands or slung on their shoulders. An old man carried a Kalashnikov loosely balanced on his shoulder and a young child followed him carrying a helmet. A man in his thirties wearing overalls lifted a revolver over his head and fired a blast of seven shots into the air.

People around him applauded, the crowd's frenzy was visibly building up. A young woman threw a cartridge belt around her neck, striding along with a defiant air.

"What are you looking at?" Arben Hazizllari asked his wife anxiously, as he got up from the dinner table. He wiped his mouth with a handkerchief and stood behind her as she began to sob quietly.

"My love, what's wrong?" Arben asked her, but she didn't answer. Tears had welled up in her eyes and her shoulders shook. He leaned forward and looked in the direction she had been looking.

The sound of gunshots grew louder. A sea of humanity overflowed into the main boulevard below. Anti-government slogans of "death" and "down with" filled the air, loud denouncements of the president and the government.

"I don't want you to go to work today," Geraldina turned to her husband. She stared at him the tears now flowing unchecked.

They were almost the same age and had met three years ago at a party organized by the military unit of Rozafa, located at the foot of the mountain with the same name. They had danced together, talked briefly and met again several times at the Public Library. They had similar tastes in reading. Their meetings became more frequent and within a couple of months they knew they were in love so were married. A year later they had a baby boy and Geraldina was now pregnant again. Their two-year-old son was sleeping in his bed, undisturbed by the sound of gunshots.

Arben looked over at the sleeping boy. He always woke him up before he went to work, singing to him.

"Wake him up. I want to kiss him before I go to work," he said to his wife.

"You are not going anywhere. Stay home. Please, Arben," she screamed at him, but he put his hand on her lips.

"I have to go. I can't desert my post and leave my fellow soldiers. It is dangerous, that is all the more reason I must go," he said to her firmly. He knew she was right, but he had to steel his resolve to do his duty and not listen to her pleadings.

"But I had a dream last night," Geraldina pleaded. "We were getting married under a roof which was on fire."

"Don't worry about these dreams. It's nothing to worry about," he pushed her aside gently and went toward the bed where his son was still sleeping.

The little boy must have felt someone looking at him. He murmured something, but didn't open his eyes. Arben moved his son's arm gently.

"Gergji, I have to go to work," he whispered in his son's ear, as the child opened his eyes and stretched his arms toward his father. Arben lifted him and threw him above his head several times, catching him close to his heart every time. His son, now awake, laughed delightedly and at that moment it seemed to Arben that the hotel room was filled with light. He held his son in his arms and walked around the room with joy in the moment. He kissed the soft cheek, nuzzling against his neck, breathing in the baby's scent, reluctant to break this contact with his child. But he did and handed him over to his wife, who was choking on her tears.

Arben put on his military uniform and his officer's hat. He checked himself in the mirror, stood to attention and saluted his image. He was proud of the uniform and had been one of the best students in the military academy and was now a lieutenant. He knew the danger that came with wearing the uniform in these days of anti-government protests, but he had no option as did the soldiers of his platoon who waited for their new lieutenant.

"Relax, my love. I'll be home tomorrow morning. Don't worry. I'm bringing two thousand leks with me to buy you a gift for your birthday," he said and kissed his wife on her lips.

He hugged his son one more time, kissed him once again, this time on his forehead. He opened the safety box, took out his military pistol, checked the safety catch and stuck it into his holster. These days military personnel were always on high alert when out in public.

Arben left the apartment, closed the door behind him without turning his head and hurried down the hallway, feeling his wife's anguished eyes on him.

It was 9 p.m. when soldier Agron Kurti came into the commander's office with his military rifle slung over his shoulder. A blue vein was pumping in his forehead and his eyes were bloodshot. Captain Martin Doda and Lieutenant Arben Hazizllari were studying the location of the military unit on the map when Kurti rapped on the door and entered on command.

"Commander, three people from the Military Police want to inspect our facilities," Kurti reported.

Captain Doda glanced across at his lieutenant then put on his hat and went outside. Arben Hazizllari hurried to follow his superior. They saw three men in blue intelligence uniforms standing beside a military van. Captain Doda noticed that they were well-groomed and their uniforms well-pressed. All three of them had pistols in their holsters. Yet Doda doubted that they were from the special police. It seemed odd to have an inspection at that late hour. He shook off his suspicion and turned to Arben to mutter in his ear.

"If their intention is to check if we are ready to guard this military post, we better invite them in to see with their own eyes that this unit is well-protected."

The lieutenant nodded silently, his watchful eyes never left the three visitors. The military police patrol went inside the barracks, inspecting the positions, the three outposts and then the soldiers.

"The situation is dangerous," one of the intelligence officers said to Captain Doda. "Be careful."

The inspection patrol left the unit immediately on conclusion of the tour. They left behind a feeling of unease.

"I am afraid they are not police officers. I think those men are from one of the lawless militias and are just disguised as officers," Lieutenant Hazizllari said and took his hand from his pistol. His finger had been on the trigger the whole time the so-called inspection was being carried out.

"I guess they wanted to see with their own eyes that this unit is not abandoned like the other units around us," Captain Doda replied thoughtfully. "It is true, sir. You will not take over this unit without a fight," he raised his voice, calling out in the darkness in the direction the inspection team had taken.

"As long as we are alive, it's not going to happen," one of the soldiers called out from his military position, as the others applauded loudly.

"Long live our commander!" soldier Agron Kurti shouted enthusiastically.

"Long live the commander," the rest of the soldiers applauded.

Captain Doda and Lieutenant Hazizllari saluted the soldiers and walked along the observation path beside the boundary fence. It was eerily quiet. Even the insects of the night seemed to be quiet and the darkness seemed impenetrable.

Just before midnight, they reached the northern part of the unit and were turning back towards the main unit. Captain Doda was startled when he heard a gruff voice from the bushes.

"Seize them! Drop your guns!"

Captain Doda instinctively turned in the direction of the voice, his gun drawn, but he couldn't see anything.

"We don't drop our guns for the trash of Shkodër!" he shouted.

The unmistakable sound of a Kalashnikov sounded and was immediately followed by a blast of gunshots from around the periphery of the unit. The unit was surrounded. The camp was under siege.

Captain Doda felt his throat explode, and instinctively raised his hand to find it was wet with blood. He reeled and fell to the ground, his eyes staring up at the dark sky. Lieutenant Hazizllari saw the commander fall and ran towards him, falling on his knees beside the inert body. He pressed his fingers to his neck trying to stop the bleeding, but the blood streamed through.

The Kalashnikov was heard again from the same direction. A bullet ripped through the edge of Hazizllari's helmet and shattered through his temple. He dropped unconscious beside his commander. Bullets rained over their heads, some hitting the two inert bodies. Agron Kurti was hit five times, but still managed to crawl towards his superiors and lay still pretending to be dead as he heard angry shouts draw nearer. He could hear the attackers advancing towards the barracks and the sounds of resistance fire coming from inside. He opened his eyes briefly to see men wearing black masks and holding guns rushing toward the military unit. He quickly closed his eyes as he heard someone come up to them. He sensed rather than saw someone checking the dead bodies. He felt his pockets being searched roughly, and his wallet being removed.

Kurti remained still till the gunshots and cries of the attackers faded into the darkness. He waited longer till the silence of death settled on the camp.

Agron Kurti breathed hard digging his bleeding nails into the dirt, which was wet from the overnight dew. Six hours had passed since the fatal attack. Both commanding officers lay dead inches from him. Kurti painfully straightened his body and moved closer to the lieutenant. He touched his bloody face which was frozen and felt like a plastic shield. His body was icy cold. Arben was dead. Both officers were dead.

Kurti crawled and hobbled towards the barracks, found the twelve other soldiers, some of whom were dead, others gravely injured. He went into the commander's office and with bloodied fingers dialed for help.

Arben lay in an open casket in the middle of the room, his head showing the scars of the bullet that had shattered through killing him instantly.

Geraldina, pale as death, sat by her husband's body. She had laid a white carnation across his chest. When they had brought his body to her, she had washed him in the bathtub with her bare hands like a baby. She changed his bloodied clothes and dressed him in his suit, the one he used to wear when he went out to parties with her.

A day had passed since that terrible night when she had got the news of his death. They had brought his body to her in the early hours of the morning. His body had started to decompose.

Through the afternoon wounded soldiers from Hazizllari's unit came from the hospital to the hotel where the body of their lieutenant lay in the middle of the room. They shook hands with Geraldina and paid tribute to their fallen comrade. Geraldina heard the words but consumed by grief she barely acknowledged them.

She huddled over the casket, whispering softly to her dead husband.

"When you left, I wanted to go with you," she whispered, "but I couldn't because of the baby. I would rather have died with you there than be sitting here alive without you."

Decomposition was advanced and his body had begun to smell unbearably.

"I took you to the morgue, but they would not take you in, since their freezer is broken," she told him. "Your body is decomposing fast, but don't you worry. I bought injections, which will prevent further decomposition. I had only two thousand leks, but it was enough to buy the injections. Now whatever is done can't be undone."

She fussed over the body, straightening his clothes, wiping away liquids oozing from the body.

"A couple of your friends just got in," she said to Arben as though he were just lying there with his eyes closed. "Xheladin and Paulin. They are both wounded. Xheladin got a wound on his arm and Paulin on his back, but they left the hospital and came here to see you."

She suddenly leaned forward.

"Did you say something, darling?" Geraldina asked her dead husband and put her ear closer to the lifeless face of her husband.

Xheladin could barely control his tears. He winked at Paulin and nodded towards the young widow, indicating to his comrade that he should move her away from the body. But Geraldina pushed Paulin's hand away and turned again to peer at her husband as though waiting for an answer. She had always followed his bidding in everything they did. She knew even now in death, he would want her to follow his wishes.

Arben's eyes had closed forever, his jaw was tightened with a handkerchief to keep his mouth closed and his arms were crossed over his chest. The young lieutenant looked older in death.

Geraldina waited, straining to sense his wishes, to hear his voice again.

She felt a movement against her right shoulder and a lock of her hair brushed lightly across her face. Arben used to tease her by blowing her hair lightly across her face. She turned, unafraid and expectant, looking towards the balcony window. Her face suddenly glowed with an almost supernatural light. She stared at the window. A bright light, like the headlights of a truck shone through the window and the curtains billowed inwards as if stirred by a strong breeze. Geraldina saw a human form outlined against the bright light as though someone was entering through a doorway. The figure came closer and a look of recognition came with a smile to Geraldina's face.

"I knew you would come," she said in awe. "I knew you would not leave me."

She heard his voice in her head.

"You must take my body to be buried in the place where I was born. To my parents' house in the village of Hotolisht, close to Librazhd."

Geraldina stretched out her arms in the direction of the apparition, towards the sound of her beloved's voice, but her hands touched air. There was nothing there, yet she could see him clearly.

Was this real, or was her grief and extreme fatigue making her lose her mind. She didn't believe in ghosts, but she knew in her heart that Arben's spirit would respond to her.

"I promise you, I'll take your body to your parents, no matter what," she answered. "But first I have to change your casket, because your body is swelling."

She called out to the soldiers Xheladin and Paulin.

"Did you hear what Arben said? He wants his body to be buried in Hotolisht, in his parents' village. We better hurry and get a bigger casket, since this one is becoming too small."

Xheladin gulped uncomfortably and looked at Paulin. He thought that the widow of their lieutenant was having a nervous breakdown. They began to back away towards the door when they heard Geraldina once again talking to the corpse.

"I wanted to take you to Tirana, Arben, but the Ministry of Defense said that there wasn't any helicopter available. They want you to be buried here. But don't worry, Arben. I'll find a truck to take you home," she sighed.

She turned to the soldiers, "I need a truck to take Arben to Hotolisht."

The two soldiers nodded and darted out of the room, running towards a nearby funeral home. The fresh air drove out some of the dread they had been feeling in the hotel room. As they walked their horror at the day's events struck home forcefully. It was a day they would never forget for the rest of their lives.

"We must follow her bidding quickly if she is to get back to normal," Paulin said. "We have to order a new casket first, which would be the easiest thing to do and then we have to find a truck. The sooner and the faster we do that the better."

Xheladin agreed shaking his head left and right like all Albanians do to express agreement and the dark silhouettes of the two soldiers disappeared into the darkness.

Three days passed and the soldiers could still not find a truck to carry the body of their dead lieutenant to his hometown. Drivers were scared to drive on the main roads that ran between cities because these were more often than not blocked by armed gangs who robbed and murdered travellers.

Arben's casket had to be changed yet another time as decomposition had advanced and the body was swelling rapidly and the stench had spread in the narrow hallway of the hotel. The two wounded soldiers didn't know what to do next to help the family of their superior. Death, most of it violent, ruled the city, and what poor facilities were available for burial were completely overwhelmed and had shut down. The soldiers' own situation was poor as both needed urgent medical aid for their wounds. They never complained, but Geraldina grew desperate as the days passed with her husband's body still in the hotel room. When a neighbor advised her to bury her husband in Shkodër city, Geraldina got upset and biting down on her anger explained to the neighbor that it was her husband's will to go home and not be buried among strangers.

On the third day, she could sense the growing resentment of her neighbors and the hotel management.

"I am going outside and I'll stand right in the middle of the road and stop a truck," she told the hapless soldiers. "You men stay here, until I find a truck."

For the first time in three days she left her husband's body alone. As she left the room, she sensed rather than saw the apparition follow her, the bright light and waft of air gently touching her. She turned and opened her arms to hug him, but again she could not touch him.

Paulin went to the window as much to get fresh air into the stifling room as to look for the young woman who was already standing beside the road. He felt deeply sad for her, as she seemed abandoned and left to her own devices. He didn't know how else to help her. He looked toward his friend, who had come up to the window to gasp in fresh air, and pointed towards the woman below.

"We had better watch her, see what she is doing, without her knowing that we are keeping an eye on her. She might jump in front of a car and be killed."

Xheladin rubbed his chin.

"I would not be surprised if she did that," he said. "She is talking to herself again. I am afraid that it's too late to help her."

"It's not too late to help her. We will see her on to a truck and then our duty to the lieutenant is done. You go and help her. I can hardly move my shoulder. This damn wound is killing me.

Xheladin took his pistol from its holster. He knew his uniform made him a target for the anarchists. They were told not to move around alone, but in pairs or groups when off duty.

He saluted the dead lieutenant and ran out to the hallway. He jumped the steps two and three at a time and reached outside.

Geraldina was standing on the side of the main road, waving her arms to the few trucks that passed by. Xheladin walked along the side of the hotel building in the darkness, trying not to be noticed by her. Cars passed by but none of the drivers bothered to stop and talk to her. They were all rushing to go somewhere and were reluctant to take in strangers in that time of civil turmoil.

A car sped through a ditch in the road with dirty water, which splashed on Geraldina. Her black widow's dress had mud splashes and her uncombed hair looked unruly.

"Why don't you stop," she screamed after the last truck passed by. "I am going to stand right in the middle of the road."

Xheladin saw that she was talking to herself again, and that she seemed to be trying to step onto the road but something was holding her back. He crept closer to where she struggled at the side of the road. He heard her tired voice protesting.

"Nothing is going to happen," she was saying. "It is the only way to stop a truck. If they don't stop I had better die too and all my sufferings will end."

She paused as if listening to something. Her head was turned towards the dim streetlight.

"No I have not forgotten our son," she said. "But he will be safe with the neighbor. This one in my womb should not live. Not without its father's love."

She stepped slowly but firmly forward to stand in the middle of the road, facing northward, straining to see oncoming traffic.

A big truck appeared travelling at a fast speed. She noticed the driver behind the wheel waving frantically at her telling her to move out of the way. She didn't move, but put her hand up to stop him.

As Xheladin watched transfixed, he saw what he later related to his friends as the weirdest thing he had ever seen. He had put one foot forward to go pull the woman to safety as he watched the horrified driver waving her frantically out of the way. Geraldina was straining away to her left as if something was holding on to her right arm and trying to pull her away.

"I told you, I am not leaving," she was screaming. "If I have to die, I better die now."

The sound of airbrakes and the screeching of tires split the evening air as the driver struggled to stop the big vehicle from running the woman over. A wave of muck seemed to rise up from the tires of the truck, and this, said Xheladin to his buddies later, was where the weird thing happened. The wave of muck seemed to gather in front of the vehicle and seemed to hold the truck back like a barrier. Xheladin was sure if it had not been for that barrier the driver would never have stopped in time and would have mowed the woman down.

The muck settled in a huge puddle and the driver stumbled out of the cab of the truck, his face covered with black dust and bruises.

"What the hell is wrong with you? Are you mad?" he yelled at her. "Why are you standing in the middle of the road?" The driver had heavy facial hair, his moustache large and unruly and his black curly hair falling in a rough mane to his shoulders.

"My husband was killed three days ago," Geraldina pleaded with the truck driver. "He was a brave soldier, a lieutenant in the military unit stationed here in this damned city. I have to find a truck to take his body home to his village."

The driver's anger seemed to visibly subside. He scratched his head with his dirty fingers and pulled at his moustaches.

"So, your husband was killed. Why can't you bury him here?"

"It is his wish to be buried in his village. His body is swelling. I can't keep him like that any longer."

"I am sorry to hear that, ma'am, but I can't help you. There are many roadblocks on the highway. As soon as you leave the city the danger from armed gangs is greater and they have set up roadblocks. They attack and steal from whoever comes along. You will not be able to get past Lezha city. The gangs there are the worst. I heard they shoot people if they resist. And you, a woman! To be honest with you, I don't dare to go there myself," the driver said.

"Please help me, Sir. How much money do you want to help me? I know it's dangerous, but I must go. Please help me, if you believe in God then I pray that God bless you and your children." Geraldina clutched his arm in desperation.

The driver didn't know what to say, his eyes suddenly focused behind her.

"God will help us get there safely. I'll never forget it, if you help me," she begged, but the driver's attention was caught by something else.

Geraldina thought he had seen Arben's ghost behind her, and didn't realize that Xheladin was standing behind her, pointing his pistol at the driver. When she turned to look behind her she finally saw Xheladin holding the gun.

"You give her the truck now, if you don't want to get killed," Xheladin warned him.

"I don't want trouble," the driver relented. "But I will give you the truck to drive. I can't come with you. I have kids, you know?"

Xheladin stood beside her and lowered the gun.

"I'll be with her," Xheladin said. "You will not have any problem. May God bless you and don't worry. We will be very careful. As soon as we finish, we will bring the truck back to you."

Geraldina smiled a little for the first time in four days.

"Alright, make sure you bring this back safely," the driver said and handed the keys to her. "Who is going to be the driver?" he asked looking at both with mistrust.

"I am going to drive the truck," Geraldina said.

"You?"

"Yes, me."

"Why can't he drive?" he nodded at Xheladin.

"He is wounded. I can drive the truck myself."

"But can you drive a truck?"

"I have a driver's license. I drove the military van several times, when I visited my husband at his work," she said.

"I can second that. I have seen her drive a big vehicle. Now give us your phone number and your home address and tomorrow night we will be back right here to return your truck." Xheladin looked more confident than he felt. He turned to Geraldina. "Right, madam?"

"Right!" she affirmed.

The driver shrugged reluctantly.

"OK. Where is the dead body?

"In that hotel," said Geraldina pointing. Her relief made her suddenly weak.

"OK, let's get you on the road if you are to make this trip and back," said the truck driver as he moved towards the hotel.

"God bless you, man," Xheladin said to him. "What about your son?" he asked Geraldina.

"I am going to take him with me," she said. She jumped into the cab of the truck, adjusted the mirrors and seat, put the key in the ignition. She turned the key and the engine roared to life. Both men stepped back and watched her drive the huge vehicle off the road towards the parking lot of the hotel. She stopped, shut off the engine and jumped down.

"I can't believe that she really can drive that!" the truck driver shook his head in amazement.

"I told you she could," said an equally amazed Xheladin.

The Boss fired several times into the air to stop the huge blue truck coming towards the roadblock his band of highwaymen had set up on the main road leading to Krrabe. At that signal, seven of his armed men jumped out of hiding on either side of the road.

The truck smashed into the sandbags, jerked up over them and hit an olive tree by the side of the road. The truck engine revved, as the driver fought for control.

The Boss waited, signaling to his men to wait. He was a tall, young man of 25, with black moustache and curly hair. He had referred to himself as the "boss' once and the name stuck as others seemed to follow him instinctively, knowing he would lead well.

The Boss squeezed the trigger once more, aiming at the driver. He stepped forward, his eyes fixed on the driver's side door. The door opened all of a sudden and a body fell from the driver's seat to the ground. The Boss approached warily to peer at the prone figure. To his amazement he noticed the driver had skin so white it glowed in the early morning light. Blond hair spilled out from under a wig of black hair. The driver's moustaches also looked odd, pulled askew by the fall from the truck.

One of the armed men had pulled open the other passenger door and looking over the driver's seat the Boss realized what the man's exclamation was all about. He saw a young boy strapped into a carrier to the front seat, who was apparently asleep. The Boss whistled to his comrades and all six of them surrounded the truck ready to open fire at the first signal. They were a hardened bunch, covered with dirt and dust from the road.

"They are both unconscious," he called out. "Bring me some water to wake them up."

One of the men went to do his bidding. He handed the Boss a can of water and watched as he threw water on the driver's face and waited for some sign of life. A pair of blue eyes opened slowly and tried to focus on the group. The Boss grabbed the black peruke from the driver's head and threw it aside as they looked in amazement at the driver who was a woman dressed as a man.

"What do you know, the driver is a woman," he laughed reaching down and pulling the driver to her feet. "A gift to us from God."

Geraldina was dazed from the crash, but she struggled to release herself from the grasp of this bandit standing grinning at her. The armed men had lowered their weapons, peering curiously at her. They had not seen women on that road in a long time. Geraldina pulled away and lost her balance, falling to the ground. As she tried to get up she was kicked from behind and fell on the road. The Boss kicked her again, this time on her ribs and the breath was knocked out of her.

The men laughed at her weakness and winked at each other, coming closer to surround her. One of the men grabbed her from behind, groping her with both hands. Geraldina screamed, whirled around and slapped him hard on his face. The man lifted his rifle to hit her with the wooden butt of the gun, but the Boss intervened, going in between them and grabbing the barrel of the gun.

Just then one of the men who had climbed onto the truck shouted to the others.

"Look at this," he called out. "There's a box in here."

The men reluctantly turned away from the truck driver and went toward the back of the truck. The Boss followed them, held the gun on his shoulder, put a foot on the tire and levered himself into the back of the truck. He saw a wooden casket draped with the Albanian flag, a red banner with a double-headed eagle. The casket was tied with rope on both sides to the truck, through all four handles, to make sure it didn't move during the trip.

A shadow of doubt crossed the Boss' face as he stood looking at the casket. Then they heard the truck driver talking to someone. The Boss grabbed his gun and leaned over the side of the truck, thinking there was another person on the scene. There was no one else in sight except the woman who seemed to be talking to herself.

"Arben, they want to open your casket. What do you want me to do?" The desperation in her voice was evident. "We are in danger. What should we do?"

"Who are you talking to, bitch?" he yelled at her, but Geraldina continued to talk to Arben who had been with her through the trip.

"Arben, do something," pleaded Geraldina.

One of the thugs leaned over the side of the truck shaking his head.

"This woman is mad. Look how she talks to herself."

"I think she is putting on an act," another said. "Perhaps they hid money in the casket and this woman driver pretends to be crazy, so she can get away with it. I think we have to open the casket."

"Nezir, go and open it then," said one of the men. "What if there is a real dead body in there?"

"We will only know if we open it," the man called Nezir said. "And you know we do not use our names around here."

As the men argued about who was going to open the casket, the Boss bent down and touched the Albanian flag with his fingers. He was bending over the casket and suddenly smelled the stench coming from it. He gagged, ran over to the side of the truck and spat on the ground with distaste.

"Who is this dead man?" he asked Geraldina.

"It is my husband," she replied.

"Why did you cover him with the flag? What did he do, when he was alive? Was he a policeman?"

"If he was a policeman, the police would have taken care of him, not left me to do it."

"What did he do before he died? Was he a military officer?"

"He is dead now. He is dead. Killed by you senseless, godless people. Leave him alone. Leave us alone. May God damn you all." She cursed them.

"Where are you taking him to?"

"I am taking him to his parents in Hotolisht."

"The smell is really bad."

"His body is swollen. He died three days ago."

"Do you have money with you?"

"No I don't. I spent all my money to take care of him."

"Who is the boy?"

"That's my son. Let us go. Please. His body can't be left unburied any longer."

"We have to open the casket, and then you can go," the Boss ordered as Geraldina began to wring her hands, tears falling down her cheeks.

"Why were you disguised like a man?" he asked her jumping down from the truck. He pulled her by the hair and shook her. "Why are you dressed like a man?"

"I dressed like that so people like you would not bother me," she responded.

The Boss pushed her again and she fell on the road. He put his foot on the tire, jumped back into the truck and walked around the casket. He winked to one of his men and indicated that he open the casket.

The man opened the lid of the casket slowly. Putrid vapours rose from the decomposing mass inside the coffin. In terror the men watched as the vapours rose to take the form of a man.

Geraldina screamed and as they jerked their heads towards her, the lid of the casket fell and closed by itself.

The Boss jumped backwards trying desperately to hold on to his courage because he knew his men were watching him, unsure of the situation.

"Let us take the woman and go," he ordered but his hands had started to shake. He felt terror rise up to his throat as though a pair of invisible hands were choking him. He gasped, choked, grabbed at his neck, his nails tearing into his flesh. He fell off the truck on to the ground unconscious.

The men stared terrified. Was the Boss having a fit? Was it a heart attack? Something strange was happening.

Suddenly the thug called Nezir who had lifted the lid of the casket felt his throat tighten, as though being squeezed by a pair of invisible hands. He struggled, falling off the truck on to the road. He was dead, foaming at the mouth, before he hit the road.

"I can't stand this smell. This is cursed. Let's get out of here," yelled one of the other men. The men jumped off the truck and ran off into the woods beyond the road.

Geraldina felt a gentle touch on her bruises, smoothing away the pain. Her hair blew gently into her face and suddenly she was not afraid anymore.

"Now we can go home." She felt the words gentle on her ear.

# The Sniper

I balanced the gun on the ledge and peered through the eyepiece at the main entrance of the casino in the outskirts of Toronto. Steadying my breath, I flexed the finger that lay against the trigger. In the last ten minutes no one had come out of the casino. The night air was still warm, even though it was early September. The hair at my nape stood up prickly with tension and my eyes were blurry with tears. I forced myself to relax and settled back waiting for the right moment.

I had climbed to the roof of this building across from the casino at three o'clock in the morning, when not a soul was around to see me. I had never shot anybody in my life. I can't remember having killed anything. I've never had any vices. I never smoked or drank alcohol or ingested any narcotic. I lived a normal, ordinary life. That was me, ordinary, when I lived in Vietnam.

My name is Lee Phang and I came to Canada with my wife Lu ten years ago. Since I didn't speak English very well at the time, I ended up working in the kitchen at the Monte Carlo, where I did not need to talk to anybody.

I knew my job. Clean, clean and clean. It was at the Monte Carlo that for the first time in my life I saw the slot machines, those evil temptresses that swallowed money. Hard-earned money of hard-working people like me, who were caught in the web of gambling, lured by the promise of getting rich.

I never understood why some people got licenses to use these metal beasts to destroy others, turn them crazy, so crazy that instead of getting what was promised—huge winnings—they ended up ruined.

These evil people who destroyed others needed to be stopped. No one seemed to realise how dangerous they were. I did. I had found out the hard way. I had fallen into the clutches of these metal monsters, owned by human monsters, and they had taken away everything I had and left me friendless and destitute.

So here I stood with my sniper gun on top of the roof of that high-rise building, across the road from the casino. I had planned everything, what I would do and how I would do it. I knew that whatever happened, I would never regret it because I would be creating awareness of these diabolical thieves and others would be warned.

I was married to Lu for 15 years. I had a daughter with her, whom we named Lin. Just thinking of Lin made her face appear in my mind's eye, as if to prevent me from doing what I had set out to do. I put down the gun and rubbed my eyes furiously to get rid of that lovely image of my daughter and I succeeded in wiping it from my mind.

I levelled the gun once again aiming at the casino entrance just as a fat woman came through the doors and stood directly in the target line. The woman was wearing a security uniform, and the rifle lens was so sharp I could see her face clearly. She looked to be in her forties. Her hair was tied like a ball at the back of her head. I guessed she was one of the security personnel on duty to keep the casino safe. I focussed on her closely, wondering what sort of a person she was. How was her life, her personal life and her professional life? Most of all I wondered why she worked for these motherfuckers, for thieves who were stealing from innocent people 24/7. Working for killers like these casino operators made her as guilty as them and so she deserved to die.

No one warned me "don't gamble because you are going to get screwed," when I went into the casino for the first time in my life. The casino invited big name singers and movie stars and paid them big bucks to promote their thievery. They keep one another in business, the business of thieves. The media—radio, TV and the newspapers are happy to advertise gambling, as long as they get paid. The whole system is fucked up. This damned place ate all my life savings. When I first entered the casino, I was blinded by all those slot machines, with their mouths opening and gobbling up thousands of dollars in a matter of seconds, spitting out a few hundred here and there to keep fools like me bound to the machines. That first time my fear overcame me for a moment, but a young woman who was playing beside me won a double jackpot of 1600 dollars. I shivered with anticipation and sat in front of the same slot machine. I inserted a 20 dollar bill and pulled the lever down. Three cherries rang in on one line. I got some money back. I was hooked for life.

I started gambling for the entertainment, but it got out of control and became a sickness like cancer. I started to play with my luck in a life-or-death manner. I put into the slot machines my wallet, my job, my family. I played till my last dollar was gone. I started to realise that what I was doing was slow suicide, but I was unable to stop myself and I could do nothing, except grit my teeth and play on.

I could only express my anger by hitting the slot machines with my fist, but they never broke. They were indestructible. I noticed the many security staff hovering in every corner of the casino, watching the whole area, ready to intervene, if any of the gamblers got violently crazy. I gave up and let myself slide into the abyss of despair.

I kept playing different slot machines, switching every five minutes or so, but all of them proved to be money-grabbing in the end. I kept pressing the spin button, pulled the bar down, but no winnings. The symbols on the slot machines seemed to infiltrate my brain becoming part of my consciousness, so that every waking moment was consumed with thinking about these machines and winning big. All I could think of was taking out more money from the ABM to feed those greedy ferocious metal beasts around me in the casino, who were waiting, calling out my name, ready to gobble up my money, eating me up as surely as if they took pieces of my flesh. They were horse leeches sucking my blood.

Gambling changed me. It was as if the top of my skull had come off like a lid and my brain was spinning around, uncontrollable like the spinning slot machines. I didn't know what I was doing anymore. I had no self-control. I began talking to myself. That made the security workers take note of me and they used to approach me asking in a very nice way, if I needed anything. I kept shaking my head, telling them I didn't need anything.

I was so disoriented I forgot where I was. I could not understand why my wallet was becoming empty in the blink of an eye. My debit cards were not working anymore. I used up all the allowable withdrawals and then I turned to my credit cards.

Then things really spiraled out of control. Once I didn't give a damn and withdrew three thousand dollars from my credit cards within three hours. I was charged 40 dollars for every one thousand dollars I spent. It was crazy. Fucking crazy. I wanted to blow myself up, but I couldn't stop the habit.

I couldn't explain what was happening anymore. I didn't understand why the casino was allowing its clients to get destroyed in this way. Letting them borrow on credit cards. To withdraw money for gambling from credit cards should not be allowed. It was not right. It was a crime.

I don't know at what point I began to see the casino and all its human workers protecting its criminal activities as the cause of my problems. They were responsible for this evil gambling habit that had now destroyed me. I just knew that thinking the way I did I was ready to fight with any of the workers if they approached me. I watched them closely and saw that they never walked alone in the halls, but always patrolled in groups and were always on high alert. They knew what was going on and they were afraid of us. And they were prepared to step in and intercept any of us who tried to hit back, but only after we had lost the last fucking dollar in our pockets.

I lost my money, my job and my family. I started to come home at six o'clock in the morning, when Lu had got up to go to work. Lu knew I hadn't come home in the night. She threatened me several times that she was going to call the police or leave me if I came late one more time, but I kept coming late and she never called the police, nor did she leave me. She must have hoped that one day I would change. But I never did.

So consumed was I in playing the slot machines, that I lost all sense of time. Once in a while I would check my watch. Many times I realized that I was in huge trouble, because I had to be at work at my auto garage in less time than it took to drive there if I left immediately. I had to drive across Toronto within fifteen minutes, for a journey that took half an hour on a weekend. I began to drive like crazy on those days when I was late and a couple of times I almost got in an accident.

One day I was racing to get to work when I was already late, and found myself driving on Hwy 427 at 140 km per hour, changing lanes so I could pass all the cars and trucks in front of me. That day I almost died when a huge truck loomed ahead of me as I overtook another truck. I swerved onto the shoulder entering the Gardiner Expressway with a screeching of tires and a blast of horns, and no doubt the curses and shaking fists of the truck driver and other drivers of the cars behind me. It was such a close call that the fact that I had escaped death sunk into my fuzzy tired brain. I felt my pants wet and realized I had ejaculated in my body's reaction to terror. I always ejaculate involuntarily in high anxiety situations, when I feel myself out of control.

My throat was parched since I hadn't eaten anything in the last 24 hours. I only drank the coffee served at the casino. My eyes were burning with lack of sleep. In a state of half-delirium, I asked myself: when should I end this torture, when, when, when?

I entered the Don Valley Parkway, exited at Eglinton Ave East and braked in front of the garage with a screech of tires and the smell of burning rubber filling the early morning air. I raced indoors, pulled on my uniform and just pretended I had been there since the morning. My movements were mechanical. My brain numb from fatigue and despair. I did not talk. I could not make small talk. I could not even be polite. When my wife Lu called later that day, I resented her questions.

"Lee, where have you been all night and day? At the casino again?" I could hear the worry in her voice. I didn't know how to lie to her. I felt ashamed. I felt all the more trapped.

"What is wrong with you?" I snapped at her. "Why do you keep bugging me about the casino? I went to get some parts for a car. When I came here I saw the phone was unplugged."

"Lee, don't lie to me. You can't lie to me. You have been to the casino all night," Lu began to shout into the receiver.

I could imagine her face thin and strained, but blotchy with anger spots. If I had been standing beside her at that moment I knew she would have hammered her little fists at my head. I calmed down and tried to talk to her nicely, blowing kisses to her through the phone, but she interrupted me by hanging up. I knew that she felt drawn down into this hole of despair by my gambling habit.

This went on again and again, day after day, till Lu stopped calling me at work. I did not see her for days, going straight to the casino from work and from work to the casino.

It was 9:45 am. I had to be at the garage at ten o'clock, where a client was waiting for me to fix his car. If I didn't get there on time, I would lose this good regular customer forever. I could barely stand, hardly walk. My hands were shaking. I got out of the casino, ran hobbling to my car in the parking lot. I got in the car, made sure the doors and windows were closed and then I screamed as loud as I could. There was no one at that time of the morning to hear me. The sound bounced off the windshield and sides of the car.

My eyes filled with tears of despair. I opened my wallet and took out one of my credit cards. I sat staring at it. How could I have withdrawn three thousand dollars from my credit card?

I must be mentally ill. The interest rate on that card was 18 percent. I had no hope of paying back that amount even in a year of saving. They were ripping off my scalp—the credit card companies and the casino.

I tried to rip up the credit card and could not, even when I bit into it with my teeth. I bent it out of shape so badly it would never be of use again. I took out the two other credit cards I had and bent them out of shape as well. It was the only way to stop myself from withdrawing money from them.

I forced myself to think that I would somehow pay them off, every single card, whenever I had a chance. I began to keep an eye on myself and took steps to protect myself from my worst enemy, me. I went to the bank and spoke to the manager about making changes to my account, so that I would not be able to withdraw money from the ABM machines beyond my limit. But still the sense of panic would not go away.

I knew I was to blame for this situation that had brought me to the top of this roof looking down on the place where I had lost my soul, lost everything. My eyelids were leaden, since I hadn't slept for many nights. The security woman with the ball of hair at the back of her head wasn't my target anymore. I had seen another security person coming out from the main entrance of the casino, a black man, big and fat. I brought him to the centre of the rifle focus. Then I paused again, and took out the cartridge case and checked it once again. There were ten bullets, one for each of the persons who were protecting the licensed thieves. I raised the gun again. A blonde woman walked in front of the guard and entered the casino. I thought about killing her with one shot. She was guilty too because the money she was going to spend at the casino would go to feed those vampires and keep them alive and able to ensnare others.

I had been about two hours on top of the roof and hadn't fired a single shot. Not as yet. My mind was still going over the incidents of the last few days which had led to my being on the roof. I looked down once more and through the eyepiece I saw the big fat black guard looking straight at me. Then he was gone and the casino entrance was quiet. I waited for people to come out again. I knew it wouldn't be long. It was almost 10 am. The sun glinted off my gun. I knew the bunch of losers who left the casino in the morning would be coming out any time now.

I had worked in a garage for the last three years at a minimum wage of 10 dollars and 25 cents. Alfred paid me in cash and that's what I liked about that job. Alfred liked my work and gave me the keys to open and close his shop like it was mine. He promised me a raise, but he never did give me one. He always changed the subject when I brought it up. He would cough hard and wipe his white moustache. I got in a big fight with him before I left for good. He told me about my wife calling at the shop all the time looking for me. Alfred was pissed at me that I came late to work and warned me it had consequences.

"Listen buddy, if you keep going to the casino, I'll fire you. Soon you will lose your wife too. I can't understand why she stays with you."

I wanted to kill him then, and tried to bite my tongue, literally, to keep the angry words in, but they came out anyway. My face flushed with anger and my body shook.

"What the hell is your problem?" I spluttered at him. "I can do anything I want with my money. I'll quit this job, before you fire me."

I knew I was the only worker he had and I knew he couldn't fire me on the spot without replacing me.

"We almost lost a customer," he warned. "Be careful, boy."

And then two days ago, the tension between us had come to a head. As I finished changing the oil on a car, I wiped my hands with a towel and went outside to smoke a cigarette. My thoughts then were that I could still save myself.

With some little savings I could recover the money I lost in the casino. A pack of cigarette cost me eleven dollars. I was buying a pack per week. That meant I was spending forty-four dollars per month. I decided to quit smoking. I was spending forty dollars per week on beer, which meant, I could save one hundred sixty dollars per month, if I stopped drinking. My cell phone was costing me two hundred dollars per month. I threw the cell phone into the trash and decided never to use one again. If I kept this savings up I figured in twenty years I would manage to save more than forty grand.

Alfred's voice brought me to reality.

"Hey, what the hell are you doing over there?" he yelled across at me.

I tossed the cigarette butt and ground it with my shoe. I walked back to work with the despair settling on my shoulders like a heavy burden.

Who was I kidding? I wasn't able to stop myself going to casino, even if I cut a lot of expenses in my daily routine. I was still going to blow what I had to those slot machines. I was over thirty years old, and I didn't understand why I remained a child. What did I do to God that this shit was happening to me? I really needed urgent help. This habit was working against me. I was not strong enough to win against myself.

I had everything, or almost everything I had wanted when I came to this country. I had a job and worked seven days a week, without a day off. I had never put my family, my wife or my daughter first. No. It was always the job that came first and everything else came after. I learned to do that growing up without my father in Hanoi. I had been a good worker and everything I got, I had earned with a lot of hard work and sweat.

It took about six months of reckless gambling for me to lose all of this security, my job and my family. Six months for the slot machines to take over my life and destroy me. They were ruling my life and strange and unbelievable as it sounds, they took over my mind. I began to see the illustrations on the machines moving, taking on human forms.

The first time this strange occurrence happened, the illustrations on the machines came to life and appeared as three women dressed in widows' black, jumping out of the slot machines talking to me in a sing-song chorus.

"Hello there, honey. How are you today?" the first widow was bold and actually reached out and touched me.

"Don't you understand that if you keep coming here, you are going to lose everything?" the second widow wagged her finger at me.

"I have already lost everything," I screamed at her and turned my head to look at them more closely, but they had disappeared in a flash. It was bright daylight. And I was seeing ghosts. I thought it was a hallucination because of my extreme tiredness and anxiety. I was wrong.

Another day, as I gave Lu a ride to her workplace, a crazy idea came into my mind. I had three hundred dollars in my wallet and I thought that day would be my day, if I tried to win. I could win a million dollars and fix myself up for good. The same old story was repeated. I went, I lost all the money I had and drove back to work like a madman. It was then the three widows appeared again before me. Before they could talk, I brushed them off.

"You are not real. This is a hallucination," I shouted.

My voice was so faint I could hardly hear myself. I was terrified, because this was proof that I was losing my mind. Or else I was dead and in a different world. I scratched my arm deeply and saw blood coming out and breathed heavily in relief. I wasn't dead.

"Don't you think we are real? Touch these," the blonde widow invited me to touch her breast. She unbuttoned her dress. I could see her white bra shining under the rays of the morning sun.

"Who are you?" I asked her anxiously and came closer to her. The blonde widow showed me her tongue and bit it a little bit.

"My name is Niada. This is Diada, and the red-haired one is Triada. Would you like to spend a night with us?"

I got in my car and turned the key with a shaking hand. I didn't wait for the engine to warm up, just slammed down on the gas pedal and drove fast out of the lot.

I checked the mirrors, as I was trying to turn the car. I shivered. All three women were sitting in the back seat. I could see them crowding together smiling at me in the mirror. Niada had black eyes and a beautiful smile. She winked at me as two little dimples formed in her cheeks. Diada was the short one, with black, curly hair. She looked more serious than the others. Triada had blue eyes. I stopped the car. I must be having a nervous breakdown, I thought.

"Oh, maaaan," I groaned and covered my face with both hands to escape the vision in the back seat. When I withdrew my hands and swung around to look, they were not there. I was relieved.

The next day I went to work from home. As I was working on a car, Alfred stopped in front of me and spoke in a low tone.

"I heard you were seen talking to someone," he coughed uncomfortably. "And there was no one there beside you. If you feel sick, you can go home early. We are slow today."

I could feel his eyes watching me.

"Do you talk to yourself?" he asked me all of a sudden.

I wished I could tell him about the three widows, but what was there to tell? He would just think I was crazy, since whoever had seen me talking to them had not seen the widows and had thought that I was talking to myself.

"I talk to myself to release my anger," I said at last. "I feel better that way."

Just then the phone rang and Alfred ran to grab it. I watched his face become dark with anger. He affirmed something to the person on the line, repeating "Yes, yes, you are right." He banged the table with his fist and looked towards me angrily. I heard words like "we are so sorry," "we will give you a full refund," "yes, of course, I understand." The customer must have hung up on him because he stood holding the receiver. Then he slammed it down and turned to me.

"Oh yeah? So you talk to yourself so you can release your anger? You have anger for what? Let me give you some advice, buddy. Forget everything, when you come to work. Leave your anger and your problems at home. I don't pay you to fuck up with my customers. You have made so many mistakes in these last few days it has wiped out your good record all these years. I've had it up to here with you."

"What's the problem?" I almost knew what was coming next.

"The customer just called me for the brakes. You didn't do a good job with his Honda. I don't know what to do with you, Lee. I really don't," Alfred yelled. I had never seen him so angry.

"I tried to help you, to give you a hand, but you never appreciated any of it. I can't keep you here anymore just for mercy's sake. I don't know you anymore. I can't rely on you at all," he said.

The despair was pushing me into the ground. I went to the back room without saying anything and changed out of my uniform and threw it on the floor. We had worked together for five years and I hated leaving like that.

"I am leaving," I whispered, as I walked past him.

"No, you are not leaving, asshole. You are fired," Alfred responded and turned his back on me.

I walked out in a daze. He followed me, standing in the doorway watching me leave. I sat on the bench by the side of the road, holding my head in my hands.

I didn't know how to tell Lu that I had been fired. But in the end, it wasn't necessary. She wasn't there when I went home. Both she and Lin had gone. Their things were missing from our apartment. Only my stuff was lying in the cupboards and on the table.

I was so scared, thinking that something very bad had happened to them. Panic rose to my throat, when I suddenly saw a letter lying on the table. It was from Lu saying that she had left for Vietnam and would not be coming back. She had taken Lin with her. She had bought two tickets for herself and our daughter, two one-way tickets.

Sitting in that empty apartment, with Lu's letter in my hand, no job to go to in the morning, no savings in the bank, and huge credit card debt waiting to choke me, the magnitude of how my life had changed dawned on me. The despair gave way to rage and to the desire for revenge. It was the casino that had ruined me. Now I would ruin that casino.

I don't remember how long I stayed on that rooftop pointing the gun towards the main entrance of the casino. A helicopter hovered high over the area and then right over my head. I heard shouts from behind me and heavy footfalls as boots pounded towards me. I saw bullets raining down from all directions.

When I awoke, I found myself in a dark cell, alone. There was just me. Me and the three widows, who still drive me crazy.

# ABOUT THE AUTHOR

Përparim Kapllani was born in the city of Elbasan, Albania in 1966. He graduated as an anti-aircraft gun officer in 1990 from the University of Scanderbeg, Tirana, Albania. In 1998, he graduated as a high school teacher in Literature and the Albanian Language from the University of Tirana's Faculty of History and Philology.

A prolific writer, Kapllani's most recent book in English is Beyond the Edge, a collection of short stories published in Canada in 2010 by In Our Words Inc. An English version of his play Queen Teuta of Illyria was published by In Our Words in 2008. His story "Bridge on Bloor" was published in Canadian Voices, Vol 1, published by Bookland Press.

Kapllani is the author of four books in the Albanian language and has worked as a journalist for "Ushtria," the Albanian Army Newspaper and "Shekulli," a daily newspaper. His work has also appeared in "Spekter" magazine and other local papers in Albania.

His first book, I Do Not Give My Heart to the Devil (poems), was published by the publishing house of the Army in 1995. The Albanian publishing house, Glob, published The Coin of Horror (short stories) in 1995. His drama Queen Teuta of Illyria was selected as one of the fifteen best plays in a worldwide competition organized by the Ministry of Culture of Albania, December 2002. His books in Albanian, Father's Urn, short stories and Visitors in Hades, a novel, were published in 2005 by the publishing house, Albin.

# Other books from this author:

## The Last Will[1]

1. http://www.kapllani.com

# Queen Teuta Of Illyria[2]

# Babai Ne Shishe[3]

2. http://www.kapllani.com
3. http://www.kapllani.com

# Also by P.I.Kapllani

Watch for more at kapllani.com.

# About the Author

Përparim Kapllani (P.I.Kapllani) was born in the city of Elbasan, Albania. He came to Canada in 2000 and began to put to paper his many untold stories. His most recent book is "Grimcat" -a novel written in Albanian, published by Shkrimtari Publishing House. "The Thin Line" was published by Mawenzi House in 2018. "The Last Will", a novel based on Çamëria genocide, was published by IOWI in 2013. "Beyond the Edge" is a collection of short stories published in 2010. An English version of his play "Queen Teuta of Illyria" was published in 2008. An Albanian version of the play "Mbretëreshë Teuta e Ilirisë" was published in 2014. His short stories appeared in a few anthologies such as: "Lest I forget"-IOWI, "Canadian Voices"- Bookland Press, "The Literary Connection", and "Courtney Park Connection"-IOWI. He graduated as an Anti Aircraft Gun Artillery Officer in 1990, University "Scanderbeg", Tirana, Albania. Years later he graduated as a high school teacher for Literature and Albanian Language, Tirana University, Faculty of History and Philology, in 1998.

Read more at kapllani.com.